BASTARDS

BASTARDS

Two Gay Dark Erotic Thrillers

Devon McCormack

CHEATING BASTARD

Devon McCormack

1

BLAKE

This kid is fucking amazing.

His tight hole. His endurance.

He shouts, screaming out his excitement as I hit his prostate.

He doesn't hold back. He never does.

I tug at his blond hair, yanking his head back. The mattress rocks about. On our knees, I take him from behind. He presses his hand against the headboard, which beats against the wall with each thrust I offer.

This kid's nasty. Doesn't ever ask to use condoms and doesn't really care where I've been. It's careless. But that's what I need.

His scream collapses into a whimper—a beautiful hum as it hits my ear.

I fuck him harder. The slap of my pelvis against his tight ass fills the room.

Just knowing Todd will be home in less than fifteen minutes excites me.

Fucking idiot. Fucking prude. As my contempt for the boyfriend builds, I pull back harder on Kyle's hair until our bodies are flush. I release his hair, gripping on his face and forcing his head to turn so I can kiss him. Not a sweet, tender kiss—the ones that Todd is so fucking greedy for these days. Just sloppy, wet, uncaring kisses.

This is what it's supposed to feel like. This is what it feels like to be alive.

My phone vibrates on the nightstand beside us. Like fucking clockwork. I see Todd's name flash on the screen. So eager to warn me that he's coming home. It's like he knows what I'm doing and just wants me to come and get this kid the fuck out of here.

He's so easy. So naïve. So trusting.

But I love him.

As the phone continues ringing, my arousal intensifies, and Kyle's body stiffens like he's trying to reject the growing intrusion. I screw him even harder, and like a good bottom, he screams out even louder than before, his fuss making me feel like I'm tearing him apart inside. But I guess I am. After all, I wasn't exactly liberal with the lube.

I jerk and shake as a warm sensation crawls across my body. I curse loudly, violently, and the kid must know that I'm about to spew up in him. The thought of filling him sends me over the edge. The energy rising in my pelvis causes me to jerk forward.

He whines. He's jerking himself off, and he quickly releases his own come, catching it in his hand like a good boy.

When we've cleaned up, I lead him to the door to make sure he's out of here on time. I don't ever take him farther than that, because I can't risk someone seeing us out together. Not that anyone would say anything. No one ever has.

We stop at the door, his blue eyes glistening in the daylight that comes through the wall-length windows on the other side of the condo.

He beams. So innocent. So young.

I hold his hand, because I know he likes that. That's just how I was at that age, so I can't blame him.

I kiss him softly, and as I pull away, I see a sad look in his eyes.

"Is this okay?" he asks.

"What?"

"How much we're doing this?"

"Of course it is."

"Your boyfriend doesn't mind?"

"He doesn't give a shit. He's off doing the same fucking thing."

Like hell he is, and if I found out he was, I'd rip out his throat.

"You know," he adds. "I wouldn't mind...like...sharing."

Of course you wouldn't, you nasty fuck.

"Like a three-way?" I ask.

"If it meant I got to spend more time with you, I'd be fine with that. And I mean, I assume if you guys are open..."

"Eh, we don't do three-ways."

Not that the idea isn't enticing. In fact, as I think about having two greedy bottoms needing all my attention, my dick stiffens in my pants. But I dismiss the idea and offer him another kiss.

"Don't I make enough time for you?" I ask.

"It'd be nice if you made more."

I run my hand through his dirty-blond hair.

"You're cute."

He smirks, though I see disappointment in his eyes.

"Get the fuck out of here," I say, setting my hand on his back and escorting him out. Todd will be here soon, and I don't need them running into each other in the hall.

He heads on his way, as usual.

I feel good. Real good.

I head into the bedroom and pick my phone up off the nightstand. I reply to Todd's message:

About fucking time. I miss you baby. :-(

After I hit send, I open my Grindr app and check out what's nearby.

TODD

Tonight's the night.

I slide the nozzle in my hole and squeeze the enema, filling myself.

I'm going to be ready. I'm going to be sexy, and he's going to plow me the way he needs to.

When I finish my preparations, I check myself in the mirror. Some of the muscles aren't as firm as they were the night we met at the glow in the dark paint party. I don't even remember telling him my name before we were in his car, hooking up. I'd been working out all summer before that party, though, so I had a six pack that even turned me on and a chest that I sometimes wondered if I could milk. It's not as great as it was back then, but it's still a nice body. I don't have any big pockets of excess fat, and I have a beefy chest and some serious guns that I've worked hard to maintain.

I'd fuck me. But I don't think I have particularly high standards to begin with, so I guess that doesn't say much.

I head into the bedroom.

Blake has the lamp on, and his kindle in his lap as he rests his back against the headboard.

I'm excited about surprising him. It's been seven weeks since we've messed around. Not on my account. If it were up to me, we would have fucked like rabbits the whole time. But he hasn't been the same since six months ago when one of his nuts had to be removed. Testicular cancer. Fortunately for him, non-aggressive, but even with the fake nut, I can tell it's affected how he feels about himself.

I haven't pressed the issue, because he doesn't need to be paranoid when I'm the one who feels horny all the fucking time.

In just my briefs, I slide under the sheets.

He's too absorbed in his book to notice that I'm intentionally wearing as little as possible in hopes of stirring his interest.

I hope he wants this as much as I do.

I scoot across the bed and lay down on his pillow, relaxing my head beside his shoulder and setting my hand on his chest.

He doesn't stir.

I know what this is. Rejection.

He shifts about. Like he's uncomfortable. He eyes me uneasily.

"I don't think I can tonight, Todd."

I feel as if my heart has dropped into my stomach.

"You said today."

"What?"

"Last week, you said you thought we could try for today."

"Baby, I'm sorry. I'm just really wanting to relax. I had a pretty hard day today."

I pull away.

I don't want him to feel like I'm making him do this.

"Is there something I'm doing wrong?" I ask. "Because, I mean, it's been a long time, and I googled how long it should be for you to start...you know."

Blake sets his kindle on the nightstand and turns to me, a sympathetic look in his eyes.

"Come here," he says.

I crawl back to him and he opens his arms. Curling into his hold, I rest my head on his chest, speckled with short strands of graying black hair.

"Todd, I want to do that. I'm not ready yet. I just don't get as excited as I used to."

My eyes water. When we first got together, it was sex all the time. We'd fuck anywhere. A car. The woods outside the condo. A public restroom.

To go from that to next to nothing is hard.

"Is it me?" I ask.

I've asked that question so many times before, but at this point, I'm pretty sure it's true. It has to be. I wish he would just admit that we've been together so long that I don't excite him anymore. Which makes me sad, because he still makes me hard as a rock.

"Todd, you are crazy. You are insane, you know that?"

I've heard those words before.

"I don't feel crazy."

"You just are. There's no one else in the world I'd rather be with. You've been with me through all that cancer shit. You were there for me when my parents were running down here to be at the hospital, even though their Southern Baptist asses kept giving you the evil eye for helping me live in sin."

I smirk as I recall his mother staying in our little condo throughout the chemo weeks, sleeping on the couch while we were in the next room. I'm sure she imagined us fornicating like rabbits, but considering he could hardly move except to vomit or take his meds, it wouldn't have been a very realistic fantasy.

"God, we've come a long way, haven't we?" I ask.

I lean up and turn to him so that I can look into his eyes.

"I love you," I say.

"I love you, too."

"You know, if you need to do anything to get back to normal, I would understand. Just talk to me. I want you to be happy."

"You're the only one I need."

Those are sweet words, but they don't solve our problem.

"I'm serious," I say. "You know, maybe a threesome would be good for us."

This isn't the first time I've suggested it. I'm desperate.

He rolls his eyes. "Todd, we're not going back over this again."

He reaches for his kindle. I grab his arm.

"I'm serious. Just listen to me. I don't think it would be totally unhealthy if you wanted to bring someone in. Someone just to play with for a bit. People do it all the time. Maybe...I can't give you what you need right now."

"I don't know how I feel about you hooking up with someone else," he says.

"I can just watch you."

I mean that. I love Blake with every part of my being. We've been together for three years. At this point, I feel like he could have three of four guys in the bed with him, and I'd be cool. Not totally cool, of course. I'd have the usual jealousy, but I could push through it. I want him to be happy. And nothing would make me feel better than knowing that he was back to his old self.

He smirks. I know that smirk. He's about to placate me. I want to protest. I want to insist that he listen. But that never gets me anywhere.

"I love you, Todd. I'm not interested in having some meaningless hookup. That's what my twenties were for. If I wanted that, I'd have stayed single."

"Okay," I surrender. "But if you change your mind...if you do happen to see something you like...or whatever. Just talk to me. Promise me you'll say something. I don't want to end up being the guy who's making you miserable. I don't want you regretting us being together because I can't give you what you need. You know that's what happened with Jeremy."

My ex who I was with for five years. Unfortunately, only two of those had any sex at all. And a lot of that is playing into my feelings with Blake, because I worry he isn't admitting that the magic is dead. It would make sense if it was.

"Considering all that you've been through, maybe somewhere in your mind, you associate me with the cancer. Maybe, whether you're willing to admit it or not, that's the reason why you can't get turned on by me."

"Are you fucking kidding me?" Again, he's looking at me like I'm insane. I know he thinks looking at me like that helps, but it doesn't. It makes me feel like a stupid kid. "Todd, you are hot as hell."

He moves toward me and wraps his arm around me, caressing my back, assessing my body. The attention is nice, but it's sad knowing that this isn't going to turn into more.

"You're everything I need," he assures me. "We just have to get through this rough patch together, okay?"

I avoid his gaze.

He means well, but I can't help think that, like with Jeremy, he's just trying to make me feel like I'm not sexually desirable anymore.

"I'm just telling you, if you did want to bring someone in, I would be fine with that. I'm willing to try whatever we need to try."

"I know what this is really about. You have needs that you need fulfilled. That I'm not giving you, and you're trying to turn this back on me."

"No!"

"No, no. I'm not mad about it, Todd. I understand. You're projecting your own frustration onto me, and maybe that's something you need."

"I throw myself at you all the time."

"But I can't give it to you, and for me, I don't feel like I need that right now. But you obviously do. Do you need us to hook up with another guy? Because I'm willing to do that if you think that's what *you* need."

The way he says it, it sounds like a test. Jeremy used to test me like that. He asked me after the second year of celibacy if I was interested in a threesome. I told him that I was. He said he was fine, but when the moment of truth finally arrived, and I actually nabbed a guy at the bar we were at, he wigged out. Threw a fucking fit. Nearly broke up with me. We should have broken up that night, but I was a fucking idiot. So we kept it going for far too long.

"Blake, I don't need that. I need you."

He appears disappointed. Like I've said something wrong. Like I've hurt him.

"I feel like shit," he says. "I should have fucking told you to do this a long time ago. If you need to have sex with someone. If you need to go out and get that fulfilled, you can. Just don't be shady about it, and I'll be cool with it. Is that fair?"

"That's not what I want."

He sighs.

"I just don't think I can do a threesome with you. I don't think I could be in the same room without getting fucking jealous, you know?"

That's a fair point, but here were are again. Right where we started. And I don't know when the fuck we're going to get through this dry spell.

"Come here," he says, leaning toward me and offering a chaste kiss—nothing like the passionate kisses when we first started hooking up. Once again, I feel like the magic is gone. Like he doesn't feel anything for me anymore.

I feel like shit for having disappointed him.

BLAKE

I shove him up against the wall, my cock hard within him. He's trying to scream, but I cover his mouth with my hand.

We've hooked up in this bathroom stall a few times.

Luke writhes about, clearly in discomfort since all I used for lube is my fucking spit, but he likes it that way. I imagine it hurts like hell. Fucking masochist.

I hear the door to the bathroom open, and I still. Luke settles as much as he can, but I can tell there's nothing he can do about the shaking.

This is part of what's nice about hooking up at the gym. The exhilaration of possibly getting caught.

He turns back to me, his eyes beaming with excitement.

I lean forward and lick across his cheek.

I own you, bitch.

We hear the guy pissing in the urinal and wait for him to leave before I continue pushing into Luke.

He's even tighter than Kyle.

I think about my discussion with Todd the week before.

I know Kyle would do it, and there's something exciting about the idea of Todd watching us fuck, not having a clue what we've been up to. Totally oblivious. Of course, when isn't that moron oblivious? He's an idiot if he seriously thinks any gay man genuinely hits a dry spell. That's what I get for dating a guy in his twenties.

I think about ramming into Kyle, Todd watching us, jerking off to me making that boy scream out.

I stroke my hand across Luke's abs, gripping his hip tighter as I take him, getting off more from this fantasy than from our hookup.

I could make the threesome happen. And then maybe I wouldn't have to worry about Todd stepping out. Because I do care about Todd. I want to be with him. He's a good, faithful guy. And he was there for me through that fucked up shit. He helped me with real estate. Showed a few houses for me. Ran errands while I was hooked up to a fucking IV for five hours a day. It's hard to find a guy like Todd, and I do adore him. But he's too young to get that a guy has needs. That it's not practical to expect me to just be with him. It's a fantasy. One I believed, too, but I've been with enough assholes to know that that's not how the world works. In fact, I'm sure as fuck that Todd has already done something and just hasn't told me about it. Because that's how guys are. His innocent act doesn't fool me. I've been with guys like him who run the same victim game, and while I love him, I know a liar when I see one. Those dough eyes and pouty faces don't fool me. I still love him to death. Just don't expect me to buy that, in all the time I was going through that cancer shit, he didn't stray a time or two.

I continue with my fantasy of fucking Kyle in front of Todd, and Todd playing the fool beside us.

I groan as I come inside my gym buddy.

***

"You know that thing you were talking to me about last week?" I ask.

Todd opens the brown bag of Chinese food and pulls out the boxes of fried rice.

"What?" he asks.

"A threesome."

He sets the boxes on the kitchen bar and turns to me.

I carry two plates to the table beside the bar and place them across from each other. Judging by the look in his eyes, I can tell he's concerned. I knew it. He's not actually going to follow through with this shit. Such a fucking pansy. But if he's going to suggest it, he shouldn't be surprised when a guy takes him up on his offer. Though I'm no dummy. I'm not going to let him pin this on me.

I make my saddest expression and approach him. "Maybe we need to do this. If not for me, for us...for *you*."

"Blake, don't—"

"Shh. Todd, I can't give you what you need right now, and maybe it's just the thing to spark things back to life, you know? Don't argue with me about it, okay? Hear me out. I'm not going to put this all on you, but let's just say that if either of us does need this, then maybe it'll help us out more than we now realize. And I'll take a Viagra or something to make sure I can get through it. What do you say?"

He smirks. "Oh, you'll take Viagra for another guy?"

I know he's jealous. He's really going to struggle when I bring Kyle in. And now that I think about it, I'm going to revel in him being pissed at having to watch what a good time we're having. How Kyle just begs me to give it to him.

"Maybe it'll be a good kickoff to me using it more regularly, like you suggested. I can get some from Reese."

He's clearly uncomfortable. That's what I figured. But now I feel like he needs to deal with the consequences. Worst case scenario is that we try it, and he doesn't like it. We've been together too long and been through too much for him to fucking leave over this.

"Okay," he says. "But how are we going to find the guy?"

I want to burst into laughter.

Oh, stupid, stupid, Todd.

I wonder if I'm just with him because he makes me feel so damn clever.

"How about we go out Friday night. To the bar. See if we can find someone?"

He nods, though I can tell by his expression that he's hesitant.

Don't worry, kid. I'll be doing all the work.

KYLE

I can't believe I'm doing this.

I'm excited and nervous. What if I don't like his boyfriend? Blake showed me a picture of him yesterday afternoon, after we messed around. The guy's cute and all, but what if he sucks in bed. Or what if he doesn't like me?

This was your idea, so don't chicken out now.

I scan the bar. I'm early, so I ordered a vodka soda. I'll need to get as many drinks in me as I can before this goes down.

Blake told me Todd's only hang-up was that he didn't want me to talk much. Maybe he's as uncomfortable about doing this with me as I am about doing it with him. I wonder what Blake's said about me. Has he told him I'm good in bed? Has he raised expectations too high?

My dick's not exactly enormous, so has he made fun of it?

Whatever. He wouldn't want to hook up with me if he wasn't interested at all. But what if he's only doing it because Blake suggested it...for me...because I said I'd do it. I had a friend once tell me that when he and his boyfriend were hooking up with another guy, he lost his shit and started punching the shit out of the trick. What if Todd loses it and just starts laying fists into me?

I shake that irrational worry from my thoughts. Blake would protect me. He wouldn't let his boyfriend do that to me.

I like Blake. A hell of a fucking lot. For a guy I met on Grindr just two months ago, I like him way too much. And it pisses me off that he has a boyfriend. I'd rather be able to finish up with school and then head over to his place and curl up with him in bed. Instead, I have to go back to the dorm with my straight asshole roommates who can't even clean out a sink. Fucking monsters.

I've never liked guys my own age. Always wanted someone older. Someone who had their shit together. Someone like Blake. The things that Blake doesn't like about himself—the crow's feet he gets Botox injections to hide, the silver hairs that mystically transform to a dark shade of black, the weary expression he tries to hide so he doesn't ever seem as tired as he really is—are things that I love about him.

The bar's packed.

I don't like the scene. I don't like being around all these people. I look down at my Converse, tapping one of my feet nervously on the concrete floor. I pull my gaze back up and search around for Blake. I don't want to miss his entrance.

A few minutes go by before I see him and his boyfriend come through the front door.

Just play it cool.

Blake told me that he wanted me to stay put and let them come to me. Evidently, Todd is a little nervous about it all, so he just wants us to ease him into it.

I wait at the bar while they settle on the other side, chatting with some guys they must know.

Blake looks my way and points to me. I look between him and Todd.

Todd's much hotter than the pictures Blake showed me.

His hair's blond like mine, but lighter. A shade I wish I had. Mine's so dark that I'm sometimes mistaken for a brunet. And guys will even call me out about it on Grindr. I wish I could be a brunet, but all my attempts at dyeing it haven't produced a believable shade.

Todd's shirt fits his body tight, which doesn't surprise me all that much because his chest was impressive in all those nude pictures Blake showed me yesterday.

Blake captures Todd's attention. They're talking. Surely about me.

I turn away and continue sipping my drink from a straw.

I feel bad that I even looked. Blake told me not to make a fuss. No waving. No eye contact. I guess I fucked that one up.

I keep my attention on the television screen behind the bar, which plays music videos. That gives me something to do.

"Hey, there," Blake says.

I turn to him.

"Sorry about—"

"Shut up. You didn't do anything wrong. He thinks you're really cute."

Cute? I would have preferred hot, but considering I don't have a muscle-bound body like Todd, that must be what a twink like me looks like to a guy like him.

"Thanks."

"Like I said, he's not really big on you talking. And he definitely won't want to hear about how we met or anything like that. We have rules about things like that, you know?"

"I remember."

"Okay. I've already worked everything up, so we're just going to go meet up with him and head back to our place."

"I could have just met you there."

"I know that, but he wanted to see you out first. In case he wanted to back out."

Makes sense, I guess. He probably wanted to bail if he didn't like what he saw, so maybe he does like what I look like.

Blake guides me through the crowd, to Todd, who he pulls away from the other guys he's talking to.

"Todd, this is Kyle. Kyle, Todd."

A rush of heat washes over me as Todd's gaze meets mine again, and I look away. Something about his look, and his beautiful face, totally throws me. I feel like I'm thirteen years old. It's weird, because this guy isn't as old as I typically like. He only looks a few years older than me. And with his chiseled jawline and crew-cut, he looks like the kind of frat-boy I would hate. He's even wearing a douchebag's signature look: polo and jeans.

As we make eye contact, he looks away quickly.

Has he changed his mind about me?

His hand is extended for a shake, and I quickly take it, trying to act normal.

I'm clearly overthinking this whole first meeting.

"Nice to meet you," I say, my voice higher than usual, my face hot as I blush.

His hand his so warm. His touch so soft.

There are some guys that you just have a chemistry with. You can't explain where it comes from or why it exists, and that's how I feel about this guy. With that simple shake, I suddenly want his hands all over my body.

But since he's not even looking at me, he must not feel the same way about me. Is he disappointed? Is it because I'm closer now, and he can see how weird my face looks. I like to think I'm not that strange looking, but my nose is a little too small and my eyes a little too big, so I've always felt like I look like a cartoon character.

I can't help but assess his form. His clothes fit him so well, and I can see the shape of his nipples forming in his blue and white striped polo. He makes eye contact with me again. Like he's forcing himself to. I force myself to maintain it. I want to turn away. I fear that if he looks at me head-on like this then he's just going to scrutinize me. Find things to criticize about my appearance. And this guy is way too hot to find someone like me attractive.

After our greeting, Blake puts his hands on either of us and leads us to the entrance to the bar.

I thought I could go through with this, but I'm trembling. I thought I would feel at ease with Blake there, but now I feel like I need to impress Todd. I feel bad for feeling so attracted to him. What if Blake catches on? Will he be mad? He must know he has an insanely hot boyfriend, so he should expect me to appreciate him, but what if he notices me enjoying him maybe a little too much? Will he get mad? Will he never want to hook up with me again?

TODD

Why the fuck did this guy have to say yes?

I'm so fucking hard. I think this is the hardest I've ever been in my life.

Before Blake, this was the kind of guy I was interested in. Shorter. Skinnier. I don't know what's cuter: his bright red converse, his full-rim glasses, or the tight short-sleeved button-up that fits his little body just right.

He must think I'm a dumbass for how quiet I got when Blake introduced him.

I figured we were going to hook up with some average looking guy. Someone that would give us an excuse to get off. But this kid is hotter than anything I could have picked up on my own. I feel bad about it. I don't want Blake thinking that I'm too into this kid. He'll get paranoid about not giving me what I need. I don't want him to feel like anyone else can do it for me the way he can.

Maybe once we get in the bedroom and start messing around, I'll realize that what I felt when we shook hands was just in my head. But I'm not sure. That touch and that look in his eyes remind me of what it felt like the first time I met Jeremy and Blake. I hate myself for thinking that, but there was some spark. Some silent exchange that I couldn't explain. I feel terrible that the feeling with Kyle felt the same.

When we get back to the condo, Blake is talking. I guess he's trying to make up for how silent I've been the whole time and how hard I've been working to keep from looking at Kyle. I consider offering to make drinks, but as Blake closes the door behind Kyle, he turns around and kisses him.

I tense up. Jealousy wells within me.

I knew this would happen. I'm not the kind of guy that can do this. I knew that even when I suggested it, but I'm doing this for us. But I'm wondering what I'm more jealous about. That I'm not the one kissing Blake. Or that I'm not the one kissing Kyle. I know the answer, but I don't want to admit it.

Blake continues kissing him, moving his hands up and down Kyle's body.

I stroke my hand over the bulge in my jeans, an instinctive response for how much pain I'm in right now.

I stay back, beside the kitchen bar while Blake pushes Kyle up against the door, providing him with the sorts of kisses I remember at the beginning of our relationship. Wide, wet, passionate. Kyle is eager to reciprocate.

This kid's only hooking up with us because he likes Blake.

I've never had a three-way before, but I always assumed that this is how it would be. There would be a third wheel, and that's clearly going to be me. But this isn't about me. This is about helping Blake through everything he's been going through. About reigniting his passion. His interest in me.

As much as I want it to help him, I can't help but selfishly want Kyle for myself. To kiss him the way Blake's kissing him.

Blake pulls away from Kyle and turns to me, tilting his head, indicating that I need to join.

I approach Blake slowly and kiss him. He kisses me the way he kissed Kyle, and I'm pleased because it's a sign that this is working. This really was a good idea.

He pulls away from me and returns to Kyle, kissing him softly before saying, "I think we should probably get into the bedroom before we end up fucking each other in the kitchen."

I lead the way as we round the corner into the bedroom entryway.

As I turn back, they enter, kissing and undressing each other at the same time.

Blake has always been a lot smoother than me. He's just better at picking up a guy. It's one of the reasons we ended up together. He has a talent for fucking, too. And then there's me. Awkward me. I don't like hookups. Never have. I need to get to know a guy before I'm comfortable doing something like that with them.

I undress myself and pull the sheets off the bed. At least I can do the legwork. I crawl onto the bed, but they're still making out beside it. Am I supposed to join in or wait for them to get into the bed?

Kyle opens his eyes and glances at me, his eyes going straight to my cock. I want to cover up, but I figure he's going to see it anyway.

"Oh, shit," he whispers between one of Blake's kisses.

Blake smiles and turns to me. He looks back to Kyle and chuckles. "Yeah, it's big."

I blush. "Shut up."

Kyle looks me in the eyes again, but I quickly redirect my attention to Blake. Blake pulls back and takes Kyle's hand, leading him onto the bed. They crawl to me. Blake offers a kiss. It's so nice to taste him again. To feel him with me like this. And while I'm trying to revel in our renewed chemistry, I can't help but imagine kissing Kyle. I just want to try it, and I feel bad for how much I want to. Although, why should I feel bad when Blake hasn't held back?

Blake pulls away and glances between us.

"You guys might want to kiss at some point."

My muscles tense. My dick hardens even more. I'm pissed at myself. I shouldn't want this as much as I do, and when I look to Kyle, I can tell that he doesn't want me. He appears apprehensive. Like he hasn't made up his mind about whether or not he wants to be doing this with me. But as Blake continues gazing between us, I figure we just need to get out of this awkward situation, so I crawl closer to him and lean into him. I plant a soft kiss on his lips, one that I hope will give me an idea of how Kyle feels about my participation. As our lips touch, it's as if a wave of fire rushes across my face. Goosebumps prick across my flesh.

Oh my God, his lips feel so good.

I instinctively wrap one arm around him and pull him closer as I cup the other behind his neck and pull him in to firm our kiss. The way he kisses back, he doesn't seem apprehensive anymore. And since Blake got to enjoy him so much already, why shouldn't I get to enjoy him, too? We tilt our heads either way, moving with each other, offering passionate kisses. I feel like he's quenching a deep thirst that I've had for so long. It's not like I want this. It's like I need it. Like his lips and his touch are all that I need.

He rests his hand on my shoulder. I want is to throw him back on the mattress and take him. Own him. But I remind myself that he's not just mine right now and that I shouldn't even be wanting him as badly as I do. I despise myself for too many moments that Blake's presence evaporates from my awareness.

BLAKE

It's so funny watching them try to make this work.

I lean back on the mattress as they kiss. Todd's putting on a good show. He wants me to buy that he's into this, but considering how apprehensive he was about even kissing Kyle, I can tell that he's making the best of the situation. Good on him. I'm impressed. I was expecting him to throw a tantrum when I kept making out with Kyle like that. Kyle on the other hand, is totally loving it. He's eagerly welcoming every kiss Todd offers. This kid's a real whore, so I'm not surprised.

I retrieve condoms and lube from the nightstand. Not something I'm eager to do, but I've gotta put on a show for both of them. Make them think I'm somewhat responsible. I approach them and grip on to Todd's neck, pulling him away from Kyle.

They exchange a brief look. Todd appears concerned. Although, his dick tells another story.

I recall Kyle's response to Todd's cock and chuckle. I'm eager to see him take it.

I kiss Todd, granting him reassurance that I care about him before I fuck the shit out of Kyle. I can tell by his kiss—reserved, quivering—that he's having a more difficult time with all this than he's letting on.

I catch a look from Kyle through my periphery. I can see the jealousy in his eyes. He wants me all to himself. Greedy little ass.

"Why don't I open him up for you?" I ask Todd with a smirk.

The look he gives me suggests he didn't want me to say that.

Kyle crawls around us and makes himself comfortable in his usual position, lying on his back and spreading his legs like a good bottom. I remove the condom from the wrapper, roll it on, and lube up before approaching him.

Todd doesn't move. I'm going to have to coach him through this.

He's behind us, gazing off. He has this stunned look on his face, like he's shocked he's doing this.

"Todd, why don't you kiss and rub on him while I'm fucking him."

Todd obeys and soon he's beside us, stroking Kyle softly. I'm already inside Kyle by the time he finally starts making out with him again. He runs his hand down Kyle's body, to his abs, caressing them, enjoying what I've gotten to enjoy so many times.

I wrap my arms around Kyle's legs and pull him closer to me as I invade his hole.

I wish I didn't have this fucking condom on. They're so goddamn inconvenient. Totally ruin the feeling.

Todd kisses down Kyle's body. He makes his way to Kyle's nipples. He doesn't realize how much that turns Kyle on. This kid is going to blow in no time, and unfortunately for Todd, if that happens, he's not going to get a turn.

Not my problem.

I take what's mine, watching Kyle cringe and call out. He must be loving having two guys giving him all this attention, because he's causing more of a stir than normal. He's never hid his enthusiasm, but this is just insane. And it's fucking making me hard.

I'm enjoying how Todd's rubbing across Kyle's body, kissing it. Not having a fucking clue what I've been up to. I think the fact that it's wrong is what makes it turn me on so much. It makes it even better that Kyle has fallen right into the trap I set. God, I'm good.

I should slow down. I should stop pounding Kyle's hole, but it feels too good, and before I know it, I'm shooting into the condom, wishing that I was filling this kid up, breeding him like he needs to be bred.

"Shit," I curse.

Kyle tilts his head up, and Todd turns to me.

They both appear startled.

I pull out of Kyle's hole and remove the condom.

"What?" Todd asks.

"I came already. 'Cause that was so fucking hot."

Todd smiles, but there's a sadness in his eyes. He must wonder how I came that easily with Kyle when I won't so much as touch him. I sometimes wonder why I won't touch him either. I care about him. I really do, but there's definitely not that spark that was there in the beginning.

"But I want to watch you fuck him," I say to Todd, nabbing a condom off the nightstand and tearing the wrapper open for him.

He takes it and puts it on.

He looks like a fumbling moron. He even tries to roll it on the wrong way first. But it's been a while since he's done this. Three years, so I get it.

"You sure?" he asks.

I'm going to enjoy this. Watching my boyfriend fuck one of the guys I've been cheating on him with. Neither having a fucking clue. Especially since I can tell this is the last thing in the world Todd wants. Honestly, if I thought he was interested in Kyle, I'd fucking lose my shit. Maybe even be more jealous than he clearly is of me for being so turned on by Kyle.

I crawl across the bed, to the other side and wave for Todd to take his turn.

He rubs some lube across his condom-covered dick and looks to Kyle, as if he's asking for permission. Then he pushes inside. Even with me having opened him up, it's clear he's having a much more difficult time taking Todd.

I consider joining in, but I'm eager to sit back and see how this plays out. Watch Todd suffer through it.

Todd's good about pacing himself. Better than he has been the few times I've let him top me. While he pushes within him, he rubs his thumb in circles around Kyle's nipple. Kyle twists and turns, arching his back as he cries out with excitement.

I laugh...way too loudly, because the pleasure I'm getting out of this is overpowering. And knowing how fucking clever I am to have pulled this off is exhilarating.

KYLE

He feels so good inside me.

The pressure is so fucking intense. And the way he's pinching my nipple is just right.

I reflect on that first explosive kiss. I've never felt like that with another guy. It was as if he's stirred all these powerful emotions within me, bringing them to life all at once and causing them to move throughout my entire body. I wondered if the sensation would go away after that first time, but when he kissed me while Blake fucked me, it was even better. My flesh crawled with sensation. I wanted him to touch me all over. I imagined it was him inside me instead of Blake.

I'm thrilled that Blake finished so soon, because now I can just appreciate Todd's body, his muscles casting sharp shadows beneath them as he fucks me. His face is locked in a tense expression, his eyes closed, but I'm staring at him. I want him to open his eyes. I want him to see what I'm trying to tell him. That I want him. That I need his touch. That I need him just like this. But he refuses to look at me. Surely, I can't be alone in feeling this way. He had to have felt something. When he opens his eyes and looks into mine, the lamplight sparkles in his pupils. He appears to be letting me know just how good it feels to him, too. And that only makes this pressure inside me feel even better.

I don't touch my dick. I refuse to.

I want to satisfy him first. I want him to come in me.

As he continues stimulating my nipple with one hand, he rubs the other across my abs. I'm glad he appreciates all those sit-ups I do, because I'm enjoying the gun show he provides me with.

He leans back as he continues to thrust inside me.

I want him to kiss me. I want him to lean down and grant me those lips that felt so good. That I was so lucky to feel all over my body.

Please just give me that back. Let me taste your lips.

It's silly to mentally plea to him like this, but it would be wrong to let him know just how much I need him while Blake is laying just a few feet away. I'm glad Blake is too busy enjoying the show to join in. Although, I can't figure out why he keeps laughing like a crazy person.

As much fun as Blake is, I need his boyfriend right now. Just his boyfriend. And I don't want to share him.

"Come on," Blake directs from the sidelines. "Fuck him like a man."

I'm thrilled that he said that, because I don't want Todd to hold anything back from me.

Todd looks to me, and I offer a smile to assure him that whatever he gives me, I'm willing to take. He pulls out and grips onto my thighs, rolling me onto my belly. I push my butt up, inviting him back inside, and he doesn't waste his time. He shoves deep within me so that I scream out. It was way too fucking fast. And he's so wide. As wide as a dildo I use every so often.

He leans down and wraps his arm around my neck, pulling me until my back is arched, my shoulder blades tight against his chest.

I'm all yours, Todd.

He greedily strokes his free hand across my side and stomach. He kneads at the flesh, digging his fingertips in as if he wants to find his way beneath it. He tightens his grip around my neck, restricting my breathing slightly. It makes me feel like I'm at his mercy. That how much life and pleasure I want, he has to allow.

I reach back and grip on to his ass cheeks, pulling them toward me with each thrust, letting him know that he can't be too rough with me.

I feel a sensation on my belly and I look down and see Blake's hand stroking up me.

I was so distracted, I hadn't even realized that he was coming to join in. If I wasn't so fucking turned on right now, I feel like I would be disappointed, but I'm not bothered.

Blake, lying on his side before me, slides my cock into his mouth.

I'm overwhelmed with all the aroused sensations that cover my body. I almost want Blake to stop, because I don't want to come yet. I want Todd to come.

Todd grips tighter around my throat so that I can't breathe. Does he know how hard he's gripping on? I doubt it, but I'm not going to stop him until I know for sure that he won't give me some air. Then he releases enough for me to take a breath.

His dick jams against my prostate, sending ripples of sensation moving through me.

I can't last much longer.

With his free hand, he grips onto my face and twists it toward him.

His mouth is right there, hovering beside my face.

Kiss me, please!

The thought, along with the stimulation of my prostate, increases the building pressure in my dick.

But he has to come!

I try to mentally will myself not to, but when his lips touch mine, there's nothing I can do. I cry out. And so does Todd. The jerks he offers provide me with assurance that he's spewing his load into the condom.

I shoot my load into Blake's mouth, cursing as my body is overtaken with a climax unlike anything I've ever experienced before. It reminds me of the first time I ever jerked off as a wave of heat rushes to my face and my body quivers with the intensity of the orgasm.

Todd pants into my ear and clings to me. I wish I was facing him so that I could cling back. Just to let him know how much I want to be in his arms. It's a childish thought. Considering all the guys I've fucked, I should be able to get it and leave, but there's something about him...something that I'm attracted to. I've hooked up with hot guys before, but none of them made me feel like this.

2

TODD

Kyle rides Blake as I kiss him, tasting his delicious mouth, cupping his face in my hand as I stroke my thumb across his cheek.

I didn't want it to be more than a one-time thing.

It was a terrible idea, and I fought as hard as I could to keep Blake from inviting Kyle back over, but he insisted. Said we both needed it. And it was helping him.

What was I supposed to say? I want him to get better. I want *us* to get better.

When I told Blake I didn't want to hook up with Kyle again, I could tell he thought it was because I was uncomfortable with the threesome. Unfortunately, it's so much worse than that. When I was inside Kyle—when I was fucking him—I forgot all about Blake. Worse than that, every time we've hooked up since then, I find I'm jealous—incredibly jealous—of the wrong person. I don't know what it is about Kyle. Is it his look? His cute face? His hot as fuck body? The way I feel like my flesh comes alive whenever I touch him? Whatever it is, it's wrong, and I feel guilty every time. Every single fucking time. But I don't want to stop. I don't fight Blake about it anymore, and it's because a selfish part of me just wants to spend more time with Kyle.

Even when we're not all together, I think about him. The way I know I'm not supposed to think about him. When I'm taking calls at the law office for my boss. Or running errands to the courthouse. I get hard imagining Kyle being under the desk, blowing me. Or I think about one of the many times I've gotten to fuck him since that first time.

Even in this moment, I despise Blake for being inside Kyle.

I'm a terrible person. An evil person.

When we finish up, Blake gets a call from work. These inconvenient calls come with him being a real estate agent—a job that has him running around and always on call. I can't say it doesn't play on my mind, but after all we've been through, I know I don't have anything to worry about. Evidently, I'm the one he has to worry about.

He heads out onto the balcony of our condo, leaving me and Kyle alone.

Kyle lies back, relaxing on the pillow.

He's a real trooper, considering how long he can take the two of us.

I sit next to him, thinking terrible thoughts. Imagining just rolling over to him and offering him a kiss. And another, and then having him all to myself.

"I think I'm going to take a shower," I say as I scoot off the bed.

"Todd," he says.

I stop. I don't turn to him. I'm afraid of what my expression might reveal.

It gets harder and harder the more I'm around him.

It's been two months. It should be easy by now, but when I look at him, it's like he can read my mind. He must know what he does to me.

"Yup?" I ask.

"You know, you could give me your number. I mean, I have Blake's, so I figure—"

"I don't think that would be a good idea."

"Why?"

I turn to him and his expression is exactly as I imagined it would be. He knows what I'm thinking. He knows what I'm feeling. And he was asking for my number because he feels something, too.

"I think you know why," I reply.

"You should just say it."

It's worse now that I know I'm not crazy. That I wasn't making up his interest all this time.

"Say what?" I ask.

He eyes me suspiciously, as though he's trying to read me.

"It could just be the two of us," he says.

"No, it can't. Ever."

"Why not?"

"Because I have a boyfriend. I knew we shouldn't have kept doing this."

"I don't feel bad about it."

"Because you're single. You don't have anything to feel bad about. This has to stop."

"You're not stopping this," he says, a menacing look in his eyes.

"What?"

"I'm just going to keep asking Blake if I can come over."

"Then I'm going to tell him I can't do this anymore."

"If you were going to do that, you would have already. But I don't understand why you feel bad, you and Blake have—"

The balcony door slides open.

Kyle silences, and I head to shower off.

As the water slaps against my body, guilt wells within me like Blake's cock when he's fucked me recently. I should be happy that we're fucking again. That should be enough. Why did Kyle have to go and mess everything up? We were fine with things the way they were. He shouldn't have said anything, but he articulated something I'd already felt. That what we were doing was wrong because of how I felt with him...because of how much I wanted him all to myself. It bothers me now that I know he can read me as well as I thought he could.

Of course I'm attracted to him. Those lips against mine. Those tight abs pressed up against my body. The grooves in his back as I'm running my hands up and down it. The way he tosses his head back and groans out, uninhibited as he vocalizes his pleasure. I want him more than I'd ever care to admit. But nothing can ever happen between us, because I'm not a douchebag.

KYLE

"You know, I wouldn't mind doing this with Todd."

I lay my head on Blake's chest, stroking my hand up and down his stomach, his short hairs tickling at my fingertips.

I've finally worked up the nerve to say something. I've wanted to say it for the past two months, but it wasn't appropriate, and I feared that if I let him know what I was thinking, he would realize my interest in Todd went beyond me wanting to hook up with him.

I just need to act nonchalant about it. I need to make it sound like I can take it or leave it. But I can't leave it. I won't.

Todd is at work, and Blake texted for me to come over after school, which was nice because my Psych class always gives me a headache. Something that can easily be relieved with a little tuck. I would have preferred to wait until Todd got home, but I know the only way this is going to work is if I keep on pretending to be as interested in both of them.

"What?" he asks.

I sit up and turn to him.

"Well, you guys have that agreement, so why should I just be hooking up with you? Can't I hook up with both of you?"

It's perfectly reasonable. And the idea of having Todd all to myself—not having to share him—that sounds so amazing. I wonder what he would do to me. I wonder if he would be even more aggressive.

"That's not happening," Blake says as he raises an eyebrow.

"Why not?"

"First off, I told you that he doesn't want to talk about when it's just the two of us. Like at all. But the other thing is..."

"What?"

"I don't think he likes you like that."

Oh, really?

"Can I just ask him?"

"Do you not like me anymore?" he says, making an exaggerated frown.

"Shut up. I just think it only makes sense, since we're all hooking up, if we can all hook up separately, too. It's only fair to him."

He props himself up on his elbow. The light from outside glistens across his pale flesh, contrasting with that dark, nearly black hair. Although, I detect a few specks of silver. He's going to need a refresher soon.

"Why do you want to ruin what we've got going on?" he asks.

"I'm not trying to ruin it. I just think that's fair."

Blake glances around like he has something on his mind before he says, "Okay. Since we're going on like this, I might as well tell you, he doesn't want to see you anymore. He'd rather we just not do anymore three-ways."

"What?"

"His words. Not mine."

I don't believe it. But after our conversation yesterday, I wonder if it's true. Why would he do that to me? Why would he do that to himself? I refuse to believe he isn't interested. Otherwise, he wouldn't have been all fucking awkward when I confronted him.

Is he seriously denying his feelings for me?

Whatever the reason, I feel like I'm about to burst into tears.

Rejection sucks.

Damn you, Todd.

But I'm not giving up that fucking easily.

"Now, why don't you just suck my cock?" Blake says.

I'm so angry right now that that's the last thing I want to do, but I can't show him what I'm feeling for his boyfriend. Otherwise, he's liable to lose his shit.

I look down at his erect, throbbing dick. I lean forward and slide it into my mouth.

I hate myself. Why did I even say anything? I should have kept my mouth shut. Then Todd would still let me come over.

I have to do something.

But right now, I just need to work up enough saliva to lubricate Blake's cock.

TODD

I sit on the sofa in our condo living room, watching a Scientology documentary and scarfing down a medium pepperoni pizza when I hear a knock at the door. I assume it's UPS. I hop up and hurry to the door. When I open it, I hardly have time to react because whoever's outside lunges at me.

I see a quick flash of Kyle before he's kissing me. I submit. Because it's what I've wanted so many times that he's been over here. It feels even better than normal. And

I wonder if it feels so good because I know what I'm doing is wrong. Because it's behind Blake's back.

Stop it!

I can't. I kiss back. Violently. Passionately. Recklessly.

Kyle kicks the door closed behind him as he unfastens my belt and yanks down my jeans and boxers. My cock springs free, and he hastily jerks on it.

I grip onto his arm and pull it away, but his grip is tight, and my resistance to this is nearly as nonexistent as my resistance to him coming over.

Tears form in my eyes as I find the strength to push him away.

"What are you doing?" he asks, his face red with fury.

"We can't fucking do this!"

"Why not?"

"Because I have a boyfriend."

"That is such bullshit and you know it."

I grab my pants and pull them back up, fastening my belt.

"It's not bullshit."

"I can't believe you told Blake that you didn't want to hook up anymore."

"What? I never said that."

"Yes, you did. He told me yesterday."

"What the fuck were you doing with him yesterday?"

"What do you think we were doing?"

"You fucking asshole!"

I charge him. As much as I enjoy being with him, nothing is going to stop me from pummeling his face in.

He backs away quickly, retreating until his back is against the door.

"Whoa, whoa, whoa! You're agreement!" he shouts.

I'm too fucking mad to think, but the words stop me from totally losing it.

"Agreement?" is all I can manage to say.

"About hooking up with other people."

He stares at me for a moment until his mouth drops open.

"You don't have an agreement, do you?"

My face is nearly as hot as when he kissed me when he barged in here.

I shake my head. "No. We don't."

His gaze drifts as the world I know falls apart all around me.

Tears collect in my eyes, and I know this isn't going to be pretty.

"He's been fucking cheating on me with you?" I ask.

"I thought you knew," he iterates, as though he's trying to make sure my anger stays at bay.

I shake my head again and turn away from him.

"Fuck...Fuck...Fuck!"

The tears are rolling down my cheeks before I know it. I don't want to be such a baby, but three fucking years. Through surgery...chemo...his fucking parents. And that's what I get?

I turn back to Kyle.

"I think you should probably go."

"But I want you," he whispers almost as if he didn't mean to say it out loud.

"Get the fuck out!" I shout. I hurry to him, grab his arm and pull him away from the door.

So many thoughts. So many emotions. I'm pissed at Blake. Pissed because of everything I've put up with. But scared that it's all my fault. That I couldn't give him what he needed. I'm relieved to know the truth. I hate Kyle for fucking my boyfriend. And I'm still hot as fuck for him at the same time.

I'm terrified that if I cave to my most primal impulse, I might wind up hurting him, but I can't help myself. I'm too overwhelmed to control my body right now. As I succumb to my rage, I push him back up against the door and kiss him. The intensity knocks his head back against the door with a thud. It must've hurt, but I don't care right now. I'm too busy trying to get this fucking button-up off him. What seemed adorable at one time, is now a wild inconvenience.

As I reach the last button, I'm so frustrated with it that I just tear at the placket, sending the button flying across the room. He apologizes between kisses as I undo his jean button and force his jeans and briefs to his knees, spinning him around to the door. I pull my own pants down.

"Do whatever you need to," Kyle whispers.

I spit in my palm and massage the modest lubrication across my shaft.

He pushes his ass out, inviting me to take what I surely deserve. Especially considering how much I've craved it. How much I've denied myself.

I press the head of my cock against his hole.

He doesn't offer his usual aroused moan. He grinds his teeth and hisses through them as I fight to get inside. Without lube, it's difficult. But I'm sure Blake has opened him enough for me to make my way in with a certain amount of ease.

No such luck.

I have to force myself in until Kyle is growling like a dog.

"This how he gave it to you?!" I ask. "Huh?"

"I'm sorry!" he calls out, his face turned to me, red as ever, tears in his eyes, surely from the pain.

"Were...you...sorry...while you were fucking my boyfriend?" I say between deep thrusts that I know are way too fast for him. They hurt my shaft, so I can only imagine what they're doing to him.

He unleashes a blood-curdling scream. It gives me some relief knowing he's expressing on the outside what I'm only feeling on the inside right now.

I continue invading his body, penetrating forcefully, rubbing my hands violently across his abs, his sides, his chest. Each touch is more aggressive than the last.

The angle I'm getting here isn't good enough, though. I need to be somewhere that will permit me to shove my dick as far back into this little punk's hole as I can. I turn to the kitchen bar.

It's about the right height. Only one way to find out.

I kick my shoes off, step out of my pants, and pull him with me over to the bar. He bends so that his stomach is flat against it. I'm still inside him, and I don't plan on leaving any time soon.

Sweat rushes down my forehead.

So fucking hot in here.

I pull off my shirt and continue drilling into Kyle, who grips onto the other side of the bar for support.

Is this how he took it from Blake? Or did he like it rougher? Did he like it when he felt like his hole was about to split in two. I plow into him. He's not screaming like before, so he must be getting used to my girth by now, which is a shame.

A slapping sound fills the air each time my pelvis slams into his tight ass.

His tears drip onto the bar as he profusely apologizes.

"Were you sorry when he came up inside you?" I shout.

I hate myself for how awful I'm being to him. He said he didn't know any better, but I can't help myself, considering he's allowing me to take out my pain on him like this.

I keep pushing into him until suddenly the tragedy of it all strikes me, and I burst into tears, collapsing on top of his back, my tears falling onto his cheek.

I feel his body shaking, but it's hard to distinguish it from how much I'm shaking right now.

He takes quick, unsteady breaths.

I kiss his cheek softly.

"I'm sorry," I say. "I'm so sorry."

"No, I'm sorry."

I pull out of him and step back, trying to calm myself. Trying to still the rage that lingers within me.

This is so fucking embarrassing. Taking him like this. Falling apart in front of him. Kyle must think I'm some sort of psychopath. He stands and turns to me, his dick hard as I've ever seen it. His face pale and his eyes wide, he looks like he's in shock. He approaches me slowly, carefully. He wraps his arms around me and brings his body flush with mine, kissing my cheek, as if he's asking for my forgiveness.

Even now, mad as I am—confused as I am—the heat he stirs within me is powerful. Potent.

And now I just want to be with him so that he can help me forget everything he just told me.

I kiss him softly to assure him that the rage has quieted.

He kisses back. I let it intensify naturally.

He kicks off his shoes and maneuvers out of his jeans. I lose myself in how good it feels to be close to him. To taste him. I kneel down and hoist him into the air. Not any issue, since I bench at least fifty pounds more than he weighs. I carry him into the bedroom, setting him down on the bed and gazing over his beautiful, tight body.

KYLE

Oh, my fucking ass.

It stings. God, that couldn't have been good for it. It reminds me of a time when I stuck my dildo in too deep. So deep I was concerned I might have had to go to the hospital.

I did what I had to do. Not just for Todd, but for me. Because the moment I realized what I'd done, how I'd hurt him, I knew he needed to punish me for what I'd been doing with Blake behind his back. When he was inside me like that, forcing it so fucking deep way too quickly, I felt like he was giving me what I deserved. Though every part of my body was telling me that this was wrong. That I needed to protect myself from the assault.

Todd leans down and kisses me.

It's that familiar kiss. The one that I always crave. Another teardrop hits my face.

I don't judge him. I can't even imagine what I would be like if I'd been in the same situation. And he's free to use me in whatever way will make him feel better. Whatever will bring him relief.

He wraps his arm under the crook of my leg and lifts it up, navigating back inside me.

The sting from his violent insertion intensifies as he slides inside. As I endure the pain, I can't help but hiss. It hurts so fucking much. He moves much slower, but it's still too quick. When he begins thrusting, I grip onto the sheets and let the pain ripple through me. Because even when it hurts, I like just knowing that I'm with him. There's something so fucking hot about being owned by him. Even if he's causing me pain.

He gazes down at me, his muscles bouncing as he jerks about, filling me with his shaft.

I look into his eyes, trying to figure out how he feels. It must be hard for him after what he'd just discovered about that asshole. I've hardly had time to consider how I feel about how Blake lied to me this whole time. But regardless, it's nothing compared to what Todd has been through.

He pants as he leans down and kisses me again, and I greedily kiss back, wanting to convince him to stay close to me, kissing me just like this for as long as he will.

"Todd, you feel so fucking good," I say, feeling totally free without Blake's presence or interference.

He massages his hand up and down my side. His body heat emanates across me. Warming my flesh. As his breath slides through his nostrils and covers my face as he breathes between kisses.

"I'm so fucking sorry," he mutters as he penetrates me more powerfully, his cock hitting that tender place in me. Exciting my nerves. Making the sensation in my dick swell.

I'm not even touching myself, but I feel the pressure in my cock building and building.

No! I can't come before him! I need to be there for him.

I try to distract myself, hoping it will make me less aroused, but the way he's hitting my prostate, it's clearly a physical response I can't control. And I know I'm going to explode soon.

Too soon.

I cringe as the pained sensation in my ass couples with what now feels like pain in my cock as my orgasm pushes through.

Todd's eyes widen and he grinds his teeth. He scoops my legs into the crook of his arms and plows me.

My prostate is so hypersensitive right now that it burns when he hits it, but I just have to wait a moment longer. I can take it, but I can't help screaming out my own pain as he screams out while he jerks and twists with his climax.

As his body settles, he relaxes and collapses on top of me.

It feels so good having his come inside me, knowing that he's filled me.

"How did you know he wouldn't be here?" Todd asks.

We lie across the bed, facing each other. He strokes his finger down my face. Such a soft touch. Something I need since I'm in so much pain right now.

I gaze at his face, taking in the beauty that, at least for now, is mine. His short, blond hair—that shade I wish I had—is slightly tousled. A bead of sweat slides forward from his bangs.

"I checked his phone. After he told me you didn't want me to come over anymore. He had a showing, so I thought that's when I could talk to you."

"I guess it's a good thing you came here."

It's a bittersweet acknowledgement. I can tell by the sadness in his eyes, because he doesn't really look all that happy about it. Like maybe he would have preferred not to know the truth.

"I am sorry," I say again. Because I don't think I can say it enough. "He told me that you didn't want to hear about just the two of us being together. To never mention it because it would make you mad. That's why I never said anything."

"It's not your fault." He smiled wryly. "You spend that much time with a guy you think you know, and it fucking hurts. You know? And I mean, I don't feel great saying this, but he kept telling me that he couldn't do anything. Like he was having a hard time getting aroused. What kind of fucked up shit is that? Why would he do that?"

I can't think of a good reason.

"Two months before I even met you?" he asks, but I know he doesn't really need a response. He's running through the timeframe in his head, trying to make sense of what Blake did to him. "I was there for him every fucking day. I was there when he found out about his cancer. I waited for him through surgery. I got off work just so I could take that asshole to the hospital every day for his treatments. It's just hard when you know that you sacrificed so much for someone who evidently never sacrificed shit for you."

"What are you going to do?" I ask.

"That's a really good fucking question."

3

BLAKE

I drill into Luke. It's an anger-fuck. I'm pissed that Kyle hasn't texted me back in three fucking weeks. Seriously?

He sure liked it when I was fucking him like this before. But I can't stop thinking about how he wanted me to give him Todd's number. Did he like Todd better? Did he think he was hotter? Did he like him because he's younger? He was always so fucking into it, but I didn't figure a whore like him would give a shit about who he was fucking. It's not like Todd gave a shit about him. Hasn't even asked about the kid.

Luke slaps at my ass as I slam into him in the backseat of his Corolla. That's the signal, but I don't care. I keep up my pace, and when he tries to slap again I grab his wrist and twist it.

"Fuckin' A, Blake!" he calls out. "Stop it! I just need a second."

I toss his hand aside, snatch him by his hair, yank him back forcefully, and wrap my arm around his throat. I constrict his breath. I whisper into his ear, in a way that I know he'll take me fucking seriously: "Shut the fuck up or it's going to hurt a lot worse than this, you fucking pussy."

He gags under my hold, and I don't let up. He needs to know I'm serious right now.

I have every right to be mad. Did I really get refused because some kid wanted to fuck my boyfriend?

Inexperienced Todd? That's who that kid wanted?

It's because he's younger than me. That's what it has to be. I bet Kyle's imagined himself with my boyfriend. Imagined them being together. As a couple. How dare he do that while I'm fucking him? Bet he thought I was such a fucking idiot for letting it go on while he was dreaming about being in some kissy-faced relationship with him. The fucking nerve.

I wonder if he's tried to contact Todd on his own. If they might have swapped numbers one night when we were all hooking up.

I've checked Todd's phone a few times since we stopped seeing Kyle, but I didn't see anything suspicious. Not from Kyle or any guy. Todd isn't going to make a fucking fool out of me.

Luke doesn't resist anymore. Just takes my dick as I plow into him. Knowing I have him completely as he trembles in fear makes me come. I own him.

In your face, Todd!

When I get home, I see that Todd's already set out dinner. Spaghetti and garlic bread, already set on two plates at the dinner table.

Good boy.

I've calmed down since I left Luke about twenty minutes earlier. He was pissed. I doubt he'll be responding to any of my texts anytime soon, but I don't give a shit. Right now, the only thing I'm concerned about is figuring out if Todd is up to something with Kyle. I've become fixated on it. It's grown, festered within me, until it has become my obsession.

"Hey, baby," Todd says as he sees me, a warm smile across his face. He's seemed so relaxed the past few weeks, adding to my suspicions. Is he running a game on me?

Bitch, I have run games on you ever since we got together.

I calm myself. I have to play up this act for a little while.

I offer a kiss.

After we both eat, a silence stretches between us. Long. Still. Unbearable. All I can think about is how I wish he would get away from his phone so that I can take a peak. The moment doesn't come till a few hours later when he takes a shower.

I scan through it. The messages are as useless as always, and I check the deleted messages, but nothing there, either.

Is he really smart enough to think of another way of chatting with this asshole?

I check his Facebook messenger next.

Nothing.

I login to his Gmail account and look for recent messages when I find a chat thread.

Bingo.

Messages with Kyle. I skim through them.

Days...weeks...of them exchanging messages, talking about when they're getting together. What they're going to do with each other. This whole time, they've been laughing at me, mocking me.

Heat builds in my face, and I'm half tempted to drag Todd out of the shower and ask him to explain himself.

I peruse the messages until I hear him get out of the shower.

I close the app and slide it on the nightstand.

I'm not thinking straight. Hardly thinking at all.

Is this what I fucking get after all we've been through together?

When he enters the bedroom, he has his towel around his waist and an oblivious look in his eyes. He's the dummy, not me! He's the fucking clueless moron in all this! I'll show him just how fucking clueless I am.

I raise from the bed and approach him quickly, wrapping my arms around him like the days when I liked him a lot more. Like the days where he made me as hard as any of the other guys I fuck.

He pushes away, but I assault him with too-affectionate of kisses.

"Come on, baby."

I slide my thumb into the towel and remove it.

His flaccid cock assures me that he's not into me. Now? Finally, you don't want to fuck me? Now I'm the one who doesn't do it for him. Too bad, because I have a rage-boner that's throbbing.

"Blake, I'm not really in the mood to—"

Because you've been fucking this kid for the past few weeks. Maybe it's lasted even longer than that. It's likely that they've been doing it since they started hooking up. Kyle's surely already told him about what we shared, and Todd must think this is real funny, running a game on him the way he ran one on him. Thinking that he's so fucking clever.

I shove Todd on the bed, and he crawls back, saying, "Blake, seriously. I don't want to do anything right now."

I unfasten my belt and slide down my pants to show him my dick, my pissed off dick that, whether he likes it or not, is going in him tonight.

"Come on," I say, crawling after him.

He rolls to the other side of the bed. I snatch his leg and pin it down so that he lies on his belly.

"Isn't this what you always need from me? A good fuck?"

"Blake!"

His intent is clear. He doesn't want this, but he doesn't have a choice. Not after what he did. If he's been laughing at me all this time, it's my turn to laugh at him.

I lunge forward and plant my body on top of his to pin him down. He flails his hands behind him, trying to hit me with his fists. And if his body was proportional to his dick, that might have been possible.

I wrap my arm around his throat, as I did with Luke and pull back sharply.

"Stop!" I command.

He doesn't.

I lean down and whisper into his ear, "I know about you and Kyle."

He's perfectly still, because he knows what he's done is fucking wrong. Because he knows that I'm so pissed at him right now. I spit into my free hand and slide it down to my dick, rubbing across it. He starts to fight for freedom, but I'm not letting up. He's not fucking getting out of this. The more he resists, the tighter I wrap my arm around his throat.

"You're just making it harder on yourself," I assure him as I shove my cock into him. His hole is tight as ever. I've never taken it when he's resisted like this. It feels almost as good as Kyle's.

He tries to scream out something.

"You thought I was so fucking dumb, didn't you? So fucking stupid while you were out running around on me?"

I stab deep within him and he tries to cry out, his face red, his mouth wide open the way it surely has been when he's taken Kyle's cock in it.

"I'm not the fucking moron here! You know how many guys I've fucked behind your back? You know how much I've gotten away with, you idiot?"

I'm shouting. I can tell that I'm tightening my grip around his throat without even meaning to. Digging deeper into his hole, I will be satisfied before I let him go. I'm going to humiliate him the way he's humiliated me. As I penetrate him, I shout out my rage, "You think you're so fucking clever. But you're not. Because I fucking found you out. Think you can make a fool out of me. Who's fucking laughing now?"

I hear the slaps of my pelvis against his ass, and I'm so fucking close. When I come, it feels better than any of the fucking I've ever done. I'm totally in control. Totally empowered, which is a great feeling after the disempowerment I felt from discovering Todd's betrayal.

He doesn't fight anymore, which pleases me.

I lie on top of him, releasing my hold on his throat, panting against him.

I haven't realized, but I've been crying, and a tear falls onto his back.

My rage must have been so intense that it consumed me.

I lean up, ready to let Todd know just how over we are.

He lies there, silent. I know what this means, and I realize it's from how I assaulted him, but everything seems so quiet. Too quiet for what's just happened.

I'm still breathing hard from the fuck, but he's lying there, not moving.

I turn his head.

His mouth is still wide open, his eyes devoid of life.

There's a satisfaction to this. To knowing that he can't laugh at me anymore. He lost the game. He's the fucking idiot who underestimated me.

But there's also the awareness that I have to hide this. No one can know what I've done.

KYLE

I'm on my way over to Todd's.

I'd been worried about him. We've messaged back and forth the past few weeks, and he's always good about responding, but for some reason, today he was pretty silent.

He's been struggling with his revenge plan.

The goal was simple: stay with Blake long enough so that he could show him that he'd been doing the same thing to him behind his back, then reveal the truth and get the fuck out of there. I told him he could stay in the dorm with me for a while. At least until he found a new place. I mean, if something else developed, it wouldn't be terrible. I like him. He's a cool guy, and even when we're not fucking, it's nice having someone like him to talk to.

He texted me earlier to ask if we could meet up. I'm just going to be straight with him. He needs to call off this vengeance thing with that asshole Blake. I can tell it's starting to get to him. Making him feel guilty. He shouldn't feel guilty, but there's no reason for him to put himself in that position, especially when he could be moving on with his life.

I entertained it initially, encouraged it even, but this is unreasonable.

I knock on the door and wait.

No answer.

I check the doorknob. Unlocked.

I enter, and the lights are dimmed.

There's a candlelit dinner at the table: chicken and mashed potatoes.

He's never made me dinner before, and it rouses hope within me. Maybe he's been thinking about taking things further. Maybe he wants more from me than these hookups.

I hope he's already decided to call off the revenge plan and that we can just grab his stuff and get the fuck out of here.

"Todd?" I call, searching around for him.

Where is he hiding?

I round the corner to the bedroom entry, and I see Blake sitting on the corner of the bed. He leans back on his palms. In the dim light under the chandelier over the bed, a sinister look glistens in his eyes.

He knows, and I'm not going to stick around to see what he's going to fucking do about it.

I turn back around, but as I'm dashing away, I feel something push me from behind. I fall forward, screaming out, when I feel a tug at the back of my head and then a push forward so that my head slams against the wall beside the entryway.

BLAKE

"Thanks for coming in, Mr. Bryant."

I smile pleasantly as Investigator Landon, a man with squinty eyes and a bulge in his belly that makes me think he's never done a sit up in his life, sits in a chair before me. I talked to him once a little over a week earlier after I first reported Todd's disappearance. I must've been one of the most helpful murderers he's ever worked with. I let him and the other investigator search the condo and ask all sorts of questions about our relationship. I was more honest than I figured I needed to be. Just in case they came across something that might make them suspicious. Although, I wasn't honest about some of the more important details.

Twinky Kyle was small enough that, bound and gagged, he fit pretty easily into a refrigerator box I grabbed from the local Sears. With a cart from the concierge desk, I wheeled him to my car and took him to the spot I'd selected especially for him—a wooded area I'd come across when I was showing houses in the area to some clients. With a flashlight and a pair of gloves, I waited for him to wake before I dragged him to a nearby creek and shoved that piece-of-shit's head under water while I took him just as I'd taken Todd. To let him know that he was mine and that I'd won.

"Mr. Bryant, I don't want to be the one to break this to you," Landon says, not making eye contact.

Is he onto me? Did they find something during the investigation?

They must have.

I recall pulling Kyle's face up out of the water when my work was done. His body, stiff in my arms, his gaze staring off, as if into some other world. His expression seemed to be locked in a grin, as though he knew something I didn't—as though he'd had a vision from the afterlife of my fate and knew I would get caught. That face had haunted me up until this moment.

"Thank you for your openness in our initial discussion with you. About Kyle Fraser and your...prior relationship with him before you brought him into your relationship."

"No problem. I just want to know what happened."

"Unfortunately, from what we can make out of the messages we found on Todd's Gmail account, it looks like he and this guy ended up hooking up on their own. Without you knowing. They were planning to run off together. The messages never come right out and say it, but it's pretty clear Todd was planning on leaving. The phone records that we pulled indicate that Todd had texted him the night that they disappeared. Now, I don't want to upset you, but this is pretty common."

"You think he just ran away? Without so much as a goodbye?"

"That's our best guess."

"What about his phone? Why wouldn't he still be using it? Or his email?"

He shrugs. "Crazier things have happened in cases like these," Landon says. "My guess is they just didn't want you trying to contact them. You have their numbers. You could have had access to his Gmail account. Maybe they're just trying to lay low. I remember you'd mentioned about the cancer..."

"What?" I ask, not understanding the connection.

"I don't mean to pry into your life, but a young kid going through all that...might not have wanted to break up with you to your face. You'd be surprised at how out of their way people will go to avoid an awkward conversation. My guess is that in a couple of weeks, you'll find out these kids are shacked up at some friend's place. But right now, there's just not that much that we can do. When we showed up to your place, what did we find? Missing things. His car isn't in the parking lot."

I moved that, along with his things, to my parents' place for a few days. Where will the cops never check? My parents' place in the middle of fucking Hickville, Georgia.

"As far as we can tell, everything about this looks like a kid who was just trying to get out. Likely because he'd developed feelings for Kyle Fraser."

Ever since this investigation began, I've been sweating bullets. It's like with cheating on Todd. There was always this little fear in the back of my mind that I would get caught. Like Karma or God would provide me with whatever universal justice I deserved. But as much as I got away with, it was clear there was no such thing as justice. No deity or force was coming after me. The same thing's true here. That stupid smile on Kyle's face, conceited as it appeared, wasn't laughing at me. He couldn't laugh where he was. Because there's no fucking God. No fucking Karma. Just me getting away with murder.

If only Todd and Kyle would have known how perfect everything played out. How their messages would wind up protecting me from suspicion. Those were my biggest concern. Well, those and the bodies I'd buried on my parents' property—something they wouldn't appreciate, but it wouldn't be the first time I've disappointed them.

I feel like a fucking genius.

I think back on Kyle's lifeless grin. What a joke. Who did he think he was to make that face?

My lip quivers. I want to laugh in Kyle's face. And in Landon's. Fucking idiot. I just got away with two murders!

"I'm just so sorry that this is how you had to find out," Landon says.

"Yes. Me, too."

I can't stifle the laugh. It comes out. Full force. Then it comes out again...and again.

I try to cover my mouth, but it keeps coming even as Landon's expression shifts from weary to horrified.

"I'm sorry," I insist, trying to conceal my face.

Keep it together, Blake!

However, the laughter rolls out of me as if there's something inside me forcing each laugh out. As if Kyle is in there, making me do this to reveal my secrets.

I manage to control myself long enough to say, "Pardon me, Landon. Am I excused then?"

Still, I can't suppress the smirk on my face.

Now Landon is just staring at me like he doesn't know how to respond. And neither do I. How am I supposed to keep my cool when I can't help but be giddy at how perfectly everything turned out?

It's clear that my laugh has revealed too much, though.

"You know what," Landon says, rising from his chair, his eyes squinting even more. "I'm going to go check on something real quick. Would you mind staying here for a minute?"

"Absolutely," I say. "That's fine. Just fine."

When he leaves, I let the restrained laughter back out. It echoes throughout Landon's office, haunting me as much as that fucking expression on Kyle's face.

Even if they get me, even if I was my own undoing, I can't help but enjoy that—for a moment—I duped them all.

The fucking idiots.

THE END

LYING BASTARD

Devon McCormack

1

<h1 style="text-align:center">IAN</h1>

He's gotta be here.

Jesse chats up one of the brothers beside a pair of inflatable palm trees. I should be helping him win this guy's interest, but I'm more interested in finding Brad than pledging. He didn't respond to my text last night, but I won't be dissuaded. The sex was too hot for me to believe he didn't feel something. But I can understand why he might not want to admit it.

"This is Ian," Jesse says, raising his voice in a way that I assume means, "I'm not going to do all the work here, dickhead."

The brother extends his hand and offers a smile. My gaze drifts down his ripped body to the tight speedo he's wearing for the beach-themed party. Considering how little everyone else is wearing, I figure Jesse was right when he suggested I abandon the sleeveless tee.

"Hi, Ian. I'm Tad. So you guys are interested in pledging Alpha Theta Mu?"

"We're definitely considering it," I say, though I can't hide my disinterest because I keep glancing around him.

Through my periphery, I notice Jesse glaring at me.

He'll be here, so I need to chill the fuck out. But he's been my primary distraction since our encounter at orientation.

"What makes you think you're brother material?" Tad asks. The look in his eyes suggests he enjoys his superiority over us.

The question is absurd. Everyone who's anyone wants to pledge Alpha Theta Mu. This is the fraternity of some of the most successful political leaders and entrepreneurs in the country. The Atlanta chapter is legendary for its prestigious alumni, which provides enough money that the fraternity can make college life for members one of the most memorable experiences of their lives as well as provide a Rolodex of networking opportunities that lead to some of the highest paid careers on the market.

"Ian," Jesse says, "started a nonprofit organization at our high school."

My cheeks warm. It wasn't something I would have brought up.

Tad's interest is clearly piqued as he asks, "Oh, really? What sort of nonprofit?"

"We raised money," I reply, "for a few suicide-prevention programs like the Trevor Project."

"That's really cool."

"Jesse's being a little generous. We started it together."

Jesse smiles, appreciating my reciprocal compliment.

We chat about my involvement with various extracurricular activities when I catch a guy speeding down a four-foot slide into a blue-and-white polka-dot inflatable kiddie pool. In just a pair of navy swim-trunks, those muscles—defined, cut—are unmistakable. He hops up from the pool, drenched in water, his eyes beaming with flames from a nearby Tiki torch as the water cascades down his abs. As he looks up—a smile spread across his face—I catch his gaze. His expression turns serious.

I recall his hot breath against me. His fingers moving across my flesh. His forceful entry and the angry look in his eyes as he plowed into me just a few weeks earlier.

It was the hottest sex I've ever had. I don't just want to experience it again. I *need* it again. I'm more than a little pissed that he hasn't reached out to me because I know he enjoyed it. I saw that look in his eyes as he slapped me around like a bitch. As he manhandled me. Tested my limits. He wasn't playfully rough. He was brutal. Slamming-my-head-against-the-wall brutal. I loved every second of it. When he lost control—when he punched me across the face—I saw the guilty expression he made. He knew he'd gone too far. He'd drawn blood, which I eagerly licked to assure him I wasn't bothered, but aroused. His expression let me know he was freaked out by my reaction. But then it just made him take me even harder. Beat on me like I meant nothing. I enjoyed his abuse more than any of my experiences with BDSM in the past. What we shared wasn't BDSM. BDSM is controlled. Safe. What Brad and I did was dangerous, which was why it excited me.

Behind the concerned look in Brad's eyes, I can see his desire to reenact that experience. If he wants it half as much as I do, that won't be an issue. He can only deny me for so long before caving to the powerful draw that has controlled me since that night—the one I've had to fight time and time again to keep from blowing up his phone with texts. Though even with my restraint, I know the three I've sent are way too many.

Another brother barrels down the slide behind him.

Brad breaks eye contact and turns to him. He throws his arms over his head and jumps up and down, releasing an excited holler.

My heart sinks. After what we did, how can he pretend I don't exist? He must feel guilty about his actions, but he shouldn't.

"Ian...Ian?" Tad says to get my attention.

"Sorry," I say.

"Well?" Jesse asks, his irritated expression letting me know that my distraction isn't making us look good. "Why don't you tell Tad about some of the organizations you plan to join?"

I regroup and continue offering Tad my resume. I need to focus. While I hadn't initially intended to pledge Alpha Theta Mu, since my experience with Brad, it's become my only mission, which works out great since it's the only one my bestie Jesse considers a viable option.

BRAD

What the fuck is he doing here?

I know the answer. I was his orientation leader just a few weeks earlier, when I made the rookie mistake of hitting on him. He was too fucking cute to resist. He talks with Tad. I do my best to keep from looking at him, but only because I want to look at him so much. Because I want to fuck him again.

My mind clutters with images of him stretched out across the wall of the orientation office as I took him from behind, admiring the grooves in his back. Adoring how compact his muscly body was. I dug my fingers into his flesh as if I was trying to get beneath it. I yanked his hair until I pulled him back—pulled like I was trying to take a chunk of his hair out. When I finally managed to force myself out of him, I flipped him around, hoisted him in the air, lay him on the desk, and continued fucking him. I gripped onto his throat, squeezing until his face turned red. He didn't fight me. Most people have limits. Most of the guys I hook up with tell me when it's too much. This kid didn't, and it terrified me.

There was just one moment where he gripped my hand. I knew he needed to breathe, but I couldn't help myself, and his interference enraged me. I leaned back and punched him across his face.

The moment I did it, I stopped moving. As I saw the blood running down his lip, I feared he would want to stop. That he felt violated. That he might even get me in trouble with the school for an act that I should've had the will to control. But he beamed as he licked his lip, and I knew I was in bigger trouble than I considered. The kid was dangerous because he wanted what I had to offer, and I knew what that could lead to. Still, I couldn't deny myself a moment to be with someone who could take my hatred. Who could endure the pain I had to offer.

I wonder if he still has marks that remind him of that day.

"Dude," Alex says as he fixates on my crotch.

It's rock-hard just from thinking about Ian.

He glances around. "See something you like?" he asks.

"Right here," I joke, assessing Alex's physique, which isn't bad, but he's like a straight brother to me.

He pushes my shoulder. "Shut the fuck up," he says with a laugh, running his hand through his thick dark hair.

"Let's do some shots," I suggest. I need them right now. They're the only thing that can take my mind off Ian.

We head to the bar and down a few before I turn back and see Ian talking to Aaron. If Aaron's talking to him, he must have gotten wind of some intel that makes this kid a particularly appealing candidate. Or perhaps he's just as turned on by him as I was. I'm not sure which would be worse. Aaron definitely has the tastes of the sorts of guys Ian would be into, and if Aaron develops an interest in him, it's likely he'll wind up a pledge. If that happens, I won't have an easy time keeping away. And my stiffening erection assures me of that. I have to stop this shit from happening.

"Let's go check out the newbies our little Archon's chatting up," I say to Alex.

We head over, and I sidle up beside the one next to Ian—a cute little guy with pale white flesh and freckles sprinkled across his cheeks. Though he's scrawnier than Ian, I wouldn't have a problem hooking up with him.

Ian doesn't look at me. I'm fine with that. If we can pretend that afternoon never happened, that would be great.

"What's up, guys?" Alex asks.

Aaron grins as he turns to me, and I know it's because he likes these kids. "This is Ian and Jesse. Guys, this is Brad, our Vice Archon. And this is our Secretary, Alex."

Alex extends his hand for shakes, and I offer Jesse one, but not Ian because I want Aaron to see that I don't want Ian to be considered.

Even in the dim orange glow from the porch lights, I notice Ian's face turn several shades lighter. I wonder what he's thinking. That I don't like him? That I didn't have a good time? He'd be so fucking wrong, and it's the opposite. That's why he doesn't need to be around me.

Aaron eyes me suspiciously. He's trying to figure out what I could have against someone I don't even know. I'm gonna need a good reason for my obvious insult, but for now I can get away with it.

"Jesse's a cute name," I say, looking Jesse up and down before making eye contact. The look in his eyes assures me that he's interested.

He's cute and all, but tonight he's a victim. If I fuck him Ian will get the message loud and clear: I'm not interested.

I feel Ian's eyes on me as I chat up Jesse. I feel his confusion. His frustration. It hurts me. Physically makes me sick thinking that I'm upsetting him.

But it's for your own good, kid.

JESSE

His kiss is fire, his caress warm water.

Who wouldn't want to fuck Brad Raeger? He's hot. Popular. He's the dream boyfriend of every gay freshmen who's ever wanted to pledge Alpha Theta Mu.

He shoves me against the wall of his dormitory and pushes up against me. Having stripped out of our not-so-modest swimwear, we're naked, his body as much like a god's as I imagined. I feel his girth pressing between my ass cheeks. His hands move up and down my torso as he fondles me from behind. My neck muscles tense as I twist my head, struggling to maintain our passionate kiss. He's a beast. Every movement he makes feels as though it's less about arousing me and more about claiming every part of my body. I'm just another lay to him. Another in a long series of guys he's done. That's part of what makes it so hot. That I mean nothing to him. I could have been any guy at the party—any twinky guy that he wanted to throw around and fuck the shit out of.

One of his hands releases me, and I hear a spit.

I don't want to do anything without protection, but I don't want to stop this moment either.

"I'm clean," he whispers. "You?"

I nod.

I suppose that's enough permission because I feel the pressure swell against my asshole and then his entry, which stings so that I have to bite down to endure it.

He isn't polite. Doesn't ease into me. He moves in so quickly that I wonder if he gets off on wounding potential pledges. If he likes the idea of breaking us.

As he pushes in even deeper, I open my mouth to scream, but his hand covers it quickly, preventing any sound from escaping.

Every muscle in my body stiffens. I'm scared. Terrified.

If I say something, will he stop?

He's way too big for me to fight off, and his forcefulness leaves me wondering if I could stand a chance against this nearly seven-foot god. But as he kisses behind my ear—a tender kiss, a sensual kiss—my fear dissipates.

But the pain inside me doesn't.

His hands return to their work across my abs, stroking about furiously—in a way that I know my flesh will be pink tomorrow. But it will be something I earned. Something I share with Ian in the morning: my conquest of Brad Raeger...or his conquest of me. It'll be satisfying, especially since the guy hardly looked at Ian, who usually gets all the attention. Nice to have a guy all to myself for once.

He drills into me, his shaft stinging at the walls of my hole.

I reach out to the side and grip onto the iron headboard of his bed, clinging on for support.

"Is this what you want?" he asks. "For me to breed you like the bitch you are?"

As his words hit my ear, my dick stiffens even more. My face fills with heat.

"Yes," I reply.

He pulls me away from the wall, staying inside me as he guides me to the bed and pushes me down so my chest is flat against the mattress. He pulls one of my legs up and rests it against the edge of the bed. It provides great leverage as he pushes within. Owning me. Claiming me.

His hands slide across my back, which I'm proud to say has benefited from all the days I've hit the gym. I'm not as ripped as Ian, but I'm not as skinny as I used to be either.

He pants behind me the way I imagine he would if he was in the middle of a jog.

After some intense fucking, he pulls out and, gripping onto my thighs, flips me onto my back. I'm eager to see him again. His sharp jawline. Waves of dampened, sandy-blond hair that covers his forehead. Blue eyes that sparkle with lamplight. His only imperfection seems to be a lone freckle or mole—I can't tell which—on his cheek. Must be Nature's way of reminding him that, generous as she may be to a guy like him, flaws are a necessary part of her art.

He reinserts himself. I twist and jerk about as my body struggles to take him. He should be easy to receive now that he's opened me up, but his movements are so quick that it feels as severe as the first time he pushed into me.

He wraps his hand around my throat and tightens.

"What the—" I say.

I can't help but speak it out loud because I was so startled by the move.

He settles, his beefy chest pushing out and compressing as he takes deep breaths. "Not cool?" he asks, a sincere look in his eyes—one that assures me he's not interested in hurting me.

I don't have the experience to know if that's something I want or not. Maybe if he's into it, I'll be into it.

"Oh, no," I say. "You just surprised me. Go ahead."

He eyes me apprehensively. Like he isn't sure he believes me, but I can put on an act.

He grips my throat again and constricts, watching me carefully as he pushes back within me.

He doesn't hold lightly, though. He squeezes like he's trying to keep me from breathing.

It's not something I'm particularly into, and the pain that fills my ass isn't the most arousing of sensations. I endure it anyway.

He chokes me and pushes my head back so that I'm forced to look at the ceiling while he penetrates me.

My face swells with heat. His cock feels more like an extra-large dildo than any of the average sizes I've taken before. And as my body adjusts to his girth, I feel powerful sensations rippling through me as he occasionally hits my prostate, sending rushes of energy surging through me.

The pressure in my head builds and builds as I continue struggling to breathe, but he lets up, permitting me a breath of air that I'm grateful for.

He leans down, wraps his arms under mine, and picks me up. I instinctively wrap my legs around his waist and my arms around his neck as he pulls me off the bed and fucks me in the air. I'm totally under his control. His bitch. He carries me over to a desk and pulls one arm away to throw his papers and books off. He plants me on top. My body shakes with the unstable desk.

I hear him work up a spit before spraying it across my chest and face.

He leans down like he's about to offer a kiss, which I open my mouth to receive. He spits again. This time it hits my tongue, and I swallow to let him know that I just want all of him in me. Even his come.

"You fucking dumbass," he says.

I eye him with concern.

He appears enraged, his jawline so tense I figure he's liable to stop fucking me and beat the crap out of me. My fear returns, making my muscles tighten, including in my ass, which makes his entry painful once again. It just adds to the already tender sensation of him within me.

He grips onto my wrists and pulls them over my head, pinning them to the desk.

I think he's about to kiss me, but he just licks across my lips. As he pushes in, I feel him hitting my prostate. It's so intense. And my dick is hard as a rock, and pressing up against his cut abs, so I'm liable to come any second now. I cry out as I feel the pressure in my dick climbing. It's an unsettling feeling, and I shift my legs about as I endure the unpleasant sensation that continues rising. It's like the come is being forced out of me.

His hold is so powerful that if he wants to claim me without asking questions, he can do just that.

I start to cry out because the intensifying pressure in my cock coupled with the sensation of his pushing against my prostate is just too much for me to bear. He kisses me hard, silencing me. He must be concerned about his dorm mates hearing my fuss.

He releases my wrists and cups a hand behind my neck, tightening his grip as he kisses down my throat to my nipple, where he offers teasing licks before biting down sharply enough to arouse me with a tinge of pain. The sensation is more than I can handle, and I feel the come shooting out of the head of my cock, the warm fluid dripping onto my belly.

I curse as Brad glances down to see his victory.

He leans back and slides his hand across my come. He collects it and shoves it into my mouth. I don't want my own come in my mouth, but as I see the look in his eyes—determined and filled with eagerness—I play along. Sucking it off his fingertips. Swallowing it because if this is his thing, I want it to be my thing too.

When I've cleaned his fingers off, he slides his hand down to my chest and continues plowing within me. My prostate is hypersensitive, but he doesn't seem to notice or care that I'm cringing and grunting as he thrusts even harder than before until he shakes, his face locked in an angry stare. It's like he's pissed at me. He offers a final jerk that assures me I'm filled with him. He settles. Then leans down and kisses me. As I kiss back, he licks my tongue like he's trying to get any that might remain on it.

Chills rush through my body as I recover from the fever of our passion.

Ian is going to die when he hears about this.

IAN

I make out with Aaron on the bed in his dormitory, but I'm not thinking about him. I'm thinking about Brad. Why would he want to hook up with Jesse? Jesse can't give him what he wants.

I saw the look in Brad's eyes when he punched me. He needed it rougher than what most guys can take. He needed it to satisfy some dark impulse within himself, and I wanted him to give it to me. Just the way he wanted it.

As Brad struck up a conversation with Jesse at the party, obviously with one intent, I worked on Aaron. Brad could ignore me for a while, but if I found a way into the fraternity—if I found a way to be close to him—he couldn't deny that chemistry that was so profound that we didn't even make it to his orientation advisor's office before he threw me up against a wall in the hallway and forced a strong, passionate kiss on me.

He felt guilty about hitting me. About how rough we let it get. But he shouldn't have. He didn't do anything to me that I didn't want. Because just as he wanted to give pain, I wanted to receive it. From him.

Aaron isn't a bad kisser. Far from it. I could have picked a lot worse.

I caress my fingers through his short, dark hair, feeling the warmth of his breath across my face. The scent of tequila hits my nose, making me cringe.

He nibbles on my lip. Then bites. As it smarts, my dick hardens. At least I can get a good fuck tonight. Although, all I can think about is how jealous I am that Jesse gets to feel Brad's warm flesh against him. How he gets to experience that touch. I wonder if Brad's fucking him the way he fucked me.

Aaron pulls back and gazes into my eyes, smiling a big, ridiculous smile. His aloof look reveals how drunk he is. A red glow comes from the lamp beside the bed, casting across his face, making him seem to have some menacing intent behind that smile.

"You're real cute," he says. He strokes my leg softly. "You ever done this before?"

I almost laugh, considering I've been in a far more advanced relationship than most guys *his* age. But it's a reasonable question since I doubt he meets many freshmen who are as experienced as I am.

"Just a little," I lie.

He kisses me again. Gently.

Being Archon, Alpha Theta Mu's president, Aaron could make it really easy for me to pledge, and if I'm a pledge, I'll be close to Brad. It's a selfish plot. I feel bad about using Aaron like this, but it's clear that Brad's going to make this difficult. That he's trying to deny the thing we share, which is something that only we share. Although, as I consider

Jesse being tossed around in Brad's dorm room, I feel rage swell within me. I'm livid.

Aaron and I strip out of our clothes. He lifts my hands over my head and pins me to the mattress.

As I relax, he releases my hands and grabs something from the headboard, latching it around my wrist.

I glance up and see a cuff. He looks down at me, his eyes asking a question that is best spoken. In my experience, I know that there needs to be good communication. There needs to be trust. This guy doesn't know what he's doing. Or doesn't care about the safety of something like this, but I chase those thoughts away. He's like most people. Not everyone has subbed for someone before.

I relax and nod, approving his request. He binds my other wrist in another cuff over my head.

He obviously does this to a lot of guys.

The feeling is unsettling.

I've fallen into a trap. I consider saying something. Backing out. But I can't piss off the one guy who can get me an invite to pledge and who can make my life a lot easier than it is for most of the guys who are vying for a chance to get in here.

He leans over and retrieves a piece of cloth from the nightstand, which he starts to put in my mouth.

I pull away.

I should say something. I know better. There needs to be rules and limits. This is totally irresponsible. But I silence myself and allow him to put it in my mouth and tie it around my head.

I've endured plenty of intense encounters, so surely I can handle whatever Aaron throws at me.

"Fuck yeah," Aaron says as he spits into his hand and rubs it across his dick.

I struggle to ask him if he has condoms, but the gag is too restrictive to get much sound out.

I don't want to have unprotected sex with this guy. I don't know him, and even though I haven't always been one hundred percent safe, I'm not willing to risk anything with this guy who I don't even feel that much attraction too. Unlike with Brad, who could have fucked me raw as much as he wanted without me asking questions. Because my lust for him consumed me. Because I craved him in a way I'd never craved another's touch. Because I wanted him to breed me.

I continue trying to get his attention, recalling why it was such a terrible idea to consent to him binding me like this without a discussion first—something I partially blame on one too many Jell-O shots.

As he crawls toward me, I kick my leg out before him to give him a clear indication to stop. He grips onto my ankle and pulls it back. I continue to struggle, but he just grins, as if he's enjoying the show I'm putting on for him.

I try to make a fuss, shouting beneath the gag, writhing about, but he restrains my legs and pushes his stiff cock into me.

I curse and continue struggling, but it just makes the intrusion even more painful. Feels like nails driving into me. Realizing he's not letting up, I relax into it because any struggle is going to make this worse.

The look in his eyes, drunk as he is, I don't imagine that he even understands that I'm not resisting to be playful or make it hotter. I close my eyes and grind my teeth into the gag as the sound of the springs in the mattress creak.

He clings to my thighs, forcing himself in as deep as he can make me take it. It's like sandpaper rubbing against the sides of my hole. This is what I wanted, though, isn't it? The pain? Someone violating me like this?

I endure my punishment.
I suppose this is what I get for using Aaron like this.

2

BRAD

What the fuck is he doing here?

Aaron walks down the hall, his arm draped over Ian's shoulder. With Ian's dark—nearly black—hair slightly dampened and Aaron's locked in place with however much gel is required to make the swirl at the end of his bangs, they're clearly showered up and ready for the day.

Aaron was working his moves on him before I rushed off with Jesse last night. I figured they might've hooked up, but I hoped I wouldn't have to see him again.

"How's it going?" I ask as they stop before me.

Ian doesn't make eye contact. I wonder if he's ashamed about what he did with Aaron or if he's pissed at me for how I slighted him. Whatever the reason, I can't afford to care.

"Pretty good," Aaron says with a conceited smirk, as though he's conquered the world, and I feel like he has. Because despite how much fun Jesse was, it was only hot because I was secretly imagining I was inside Ian.

We head downstairs together. Aaron strikes up a conversation about our meeting on Friday until we reach the bottom of the stairs, where he checks his phone.

"Shit. I am so fucking late. Guess we shouldn't have messed around this morning after all." He gives Ian a sly look, and I'm about to beat his fucking face in.

"You coming to the party on Friday?" he asks Ian.

He's not yours, you fucking asshole. He's mine.

I feel terrible for my possessive thought. I don't own Ian. I've been nothing but a dick to him ever since he got here, so I don't have the right to lay any claim on him. But something about knowing Aaron had his greedy, heartless paws on him just pisses me the fuck off. I know his kinky routine, and it's likely that a kid like Ian, who is so eager about what I have to offer, is all about Aaron. But as Ian glances at me briefly, I feel that he's still as interested in me as I am in him. It's something I wish I could surrender to so that I can give myself the pleasure I desperately crave. But it can't be. I know where these urges can lead, so for his sake, I have to do the right thing.

"You mind showing Ian to the kitchen so he can get a little breakfast before he goes?" Aaron asks.

"I'll be fine," Ian says like that's the last thing in the world he wants. "I was just going to—"

"Shut up," Aaron commands.

I want to punch him across his stupid face for being such an asshole.

"Just go with Brad, and he'll take care of you."

I've already taken care of him.

"I have to—"

"Brad, it'll take you five fucking seconds. Just do me a solid."

"Fine."

"I'll text you later, okay?" Aaron says, offering Ian a kiss before heading off.

A kiss. Allowing him to stay and wash off. Aaron's taken to this kid way too quickly, and that isn't going to help me any.

As Aaron heads out, Ian assesses my body. I should've thrown on a shirt before prancing around the house. Don't need to give either of us a reason to want the other any more than we already do, but now that he's looking at me like that—desire in his eyes—I feel my dick hardening.

"Come on," I say abruptly, trying to sound like the least inviting person in the world.

I lead him to the kitchen.

Several guys are lounging around. Chatting. Eating breakfast. These are just the officers and a few of the wealthier brothers who can afford to live at the official Alpha Theta Mu house. Forty-three of us total. All the guys except Aaron and me share rooms—one of the many advantages of being leaders of the house.

A shirtless Tad sits at the table, a half-eaten cream cheese bagel before him. He presses his fingers against his forehead as he hands Finn some folded up bills. Finn shouts about his attempt to pick up a girl last night as he pockets the cash. His volume is obviously his attempt at competing against the other guys' who are chatting, but Tad's increasingly tensing expression suggests Finn's words are only making his hangover even worse.

Finn fishes through his black fanny pack and pulls out a few pills that look like oxycodone and hands them to Tad. Tad downs them with his coffee. He needs to pace himself. It's only Tuesday—the second day of rush week. The parties are far from over.

A few of the other guys look just as pained and worn out, though they're dressed and ready to head to class.

I give Ian a quick tour, and I can tell he's uneasy. I refuse to introduce him to the other guys, and I can tell that they're all judging him for what they know he did with Aaron last night. There are a few who I know are homophobic. Who would be happier at Alpha Theta Mu if the leadership wasn't dominated by two of the biggest faggots in school, and if they so much as glare at Ian, I'm gonna bash their fucking faces in.

Once I've finished showing him where everything is, I say, "Help yourself. You're the Archon's guest, so you can have whatever you want."

Ian heads to a cabinet and retrieves a box of Captain Crunch. I fetch him a bowl and some milk. Help him fix his breakfast. And the fact that he chose Captain Crunch only makes me want the adorable son of a bitch more.

Ian takes his bowl and sits at the dining table, side-eyeing the seven other guys sitting around it.

I grab a mug and fix a cup of coffee at the Keurig before joining him, sitting adjacent to him at the corner of the table.

In my desperate attempt to keep my eyes off him, I didn't notice the pink marks around his wrists.

They remind me of Aaron's interests.

"You okay, kid?" I ask, muttering so the other guys won't hear me.

I don't know why the words come out of my mouth. I punched him in the face, and now I'm asking him if he's okay over some stupid cuffs? Still, I can't deny my concern about him. The idea of someone other than me laying a hand on him makes me furious.

"What do you care?"

"Good point. I don't."

I can feel my face turning red. It's not about his attitude, but because I can't get his wounds out of my head. And now all I can think about is him fucking Aaron. The idea haunts me. Makes me sick because I could have been with him instead of Jesse. Not that Jesse was bad. He just wasn't Ian. Ian was fucking incredible. I want to convince myself that it was a fluke. Some magic moment that can never be recreated, but the more I tell myself that, the more tempted I am to reenact it to see if that's really the case.

Ian eats his cereal, occasionally looking to me uneasily.

I take a sip of my coffee before asking, "What?"

"You just going to sit there?"

"I can go," I say, not moving because I don't want to leave.

"No, no."

We sit there, neither speaking. I delight in the sound of his crunching cereal as he chews.

His thick brown eyebrows need a good trim. And his resting face—a constant pout—isn't particularly attractive. The only thing he seems to have going for him are the bulges in the sleeves of the polo Aaron must have loaned him. As much as I try to fixate on the unappealing aspects of him, all I want to do is shove my cock between his thin, inviting lips. And when he glances at me briefly, those beautiful brown eyes make me forget about all the perceived faults I've found with him.

"You know, Alpha Theta Mu really isn't for you," I say bluntly.

"What?" he asks. He doesn't look confused. Just hurt.

It kills me that I have to do this, but it's for the best. Nothing good can come of him being here. Right now, I have my wits about me enough to keep him at bay, but if he keeps hanging around with Aaron, I'm not sure I'll be able to muster the necessary restraint. Especially when the only thing that keeps running through my mind are scenarios where I can get him on his own and take everything I can from him. Abuse him. Torture him the way he so desperately wants to be tortured.

"You should consider another fraternity is all I'm saying."

His look transforms from hurt to anger.

"Am I not good enough for Alpha Theta Mu?"

"I don't think it'd be a very good fit."

"You seemed to make it fit just fine, if I remember correctly."

My face flashes with heat. His obstinacy is pissing me off. Makes me want to put him in his place that much more.

"You know what happens when you kick a hornet's nest, Ian?"

"You get stung," he replies. Now he's making deliberate eye contact, refusing to let up.

"By a lot of hornets."

"Only a problem if you can't take the pain."

You are a fucking dumbass.

I want to punch him for how stupid he's being.

I glance around to make sure no one is paying attention to us. They're all too absorbed in their own conversations to notice as I lean to him and whisper, "Why the fuck did you hook up with Aaron last night?"

"Maybe I liked him. Why did you hook up with my best friend?"

"To send you a message."

"And what is that?"

"That nothing's ever going to happen between us again. And I suggest, for your own sake, you keep as far away from me as you can."

He straightens his neck. He has an air of confidence about him. Like he thinks he's the shit. And he is.

"Well, I'm not here for you...clearly. I'm here for Aaron."

I feel the impulse to bark like a dog. I've never felt this worked up about a guy before. I want to bash his face in and fuck his hole as hard as I can. But not to punish him. To give him what he needs.

I ball my hands into fists, containing the primal impulses that surge through me.

"Good luck with that," I say. "You're just another trick to him, and you know it."

"Then you have nothing to worry about."

This bitch thinks that if he can get close to me, he can trick me into doing something with him again. This isn't about Aaron. Never was. Just like me fucking Jesse wasn't about Jesse.

"Do what you want," I say. "We're probably going to keep running into each other anyway since I plan on seeing Jesse again."

His confident expression shifts to something more menacing. I've gotten to him like he's gotten to me.

He stands up and takes his bowl to the garbage disposal. He rinses the bowl and spoon before placing them in the dishwasher. He takes his sweet time, a confident look on his face. When he's finished, he approaches me and says, "Thank you for giving me the royal Alpha Theta Mu introduction. I'll definitely be considering whether I'll be pledging here."

Though he's trying to sound as though my words have made him lose interest, I know better. I see deceit in his eyes.

I rise and approach him, trying to appear as threatening as possible as I get right up next to him and say, in a low, brooding voice, "Just try, and I promise I will blackball you. You don't stand a fucking chance."

Although, that would only work if Aaron lost interest and didn't care about whether or not he pledged. If Aaron is still interested in him by the end of rush, I'm fucked.

The other guys quiet as they become aware of the tension between us. They continue talking, but I can tell they've quieted because they're eavesdropping.

"Looking forward to you pledging," I say with a smile as I set my hand on his shoulder to ward off their suspicions.

He makes a phony, knowing smile and thanks me before heading down the hall to the main entrance.

Rage races through my veins. I hurry back up to my room and pound my fist into my mattress.

I have to get it out of my system. I want to fuck him for making me feel this way. Fuck him for making me want him so bad.

I hate him for reminding me that I'm a terrible person with this dark presence within me. For reminding me of how bad things can get if I unleash this monster that I desperately try to contain

IAN

"It was so fucking hot," Jesse says.

I dig my fingernails into my palm and grind my teeth as I suppress my desire to kick his ass for hooking up with Brad. Jesse and I have always been good friends. We've never been interested in the same guys. But things are different now because he's fucking with the wrong guy. *My* guy.

It isn't his fault, I have to keep reminding myself. I didn't even let him know that I was interested in Brad. He hasn't done anything wrong, but it doesn't keep me from feeling animosity toward him. I saw some of the bruises across his body when he stepped out of the shower after he got back from his run this afternoon. I wish those were mine. That Brad had claimed me like he did Jesse last night. Just thinking that he chose Jesse over me makes me want to cry.

"Can you believe I hooked up with one of the hottest linebackers at our school?" he says.

"Are you seeing him again?"

"Yeah. He wants me to come to the party on Friday. Isn't that great?"

"That's perfect. I got invited by Aaron."

"That's incredible! We could be the boyfriends of the Archon and the Vice Archon. Oh my God, we're going to rule the roost."

I feel bad that he has such pleasant dreams about our future at Alpha Theta Mu when here I'm conspiring to take away this guy he likes. But it doesn't count as taking him away when I had him first, and when he's still interested in me. He's just scared of what we crave. I'm scared too. I'm terrified that all I want is for him to hurt me. To make me scream out in pain. To unleash the darkness within him on me until it's so painful that I don't have a way to escape it.

It's not like with Aaron. With him, I just wanted a hookup. The pain I felt with him didn't arouse me. With Brad, it was different, but I'm not sure why. Was it just our chemistry? Or because there was some beauty in his resistance against this darker part of himself? Was I just enchanted with watching him battle his inner demons— waging a war against them to protect me from their worst?

"You know how I'll look being the boyfriend of the hottest openly gay athlete at Rayden University?" he asks.

"Seems a little premature to be talking like that. This could just be what they do to newbies."

"I don't know," he says. "You should have been there. It was fucking insanely hot. And he obviously wants to see me again."

This isn't the first time Jesse's put the cart before the horse. Throughout high school, he was always the one who would fall in love after three minutes of knowing a guy. In fact, when we would go rock climbing together after school, he would frequently refer to some of the other climbers as his future husbands. As much as I played along with his little game, I could tell there was some truth behind the comment. He didn't want to hook up. He wanted to be in a relationship. But considering my conversation with Brad, I know he's just going to use Jesse to keep me at bay. And that won't work.

3

IAN

"Come in me. Come in me, please!" I beg Aaron because I know that's what he wants.

It's Sunday. Rush week is over, and today, the brothers place bids on new pledges for who they want to join Alpha Theta Mu, so this performance is critical.

Aaron snuck me into his room earlier because brothers aren't allowed to fraternize with any potential pledges before the bid meeting. I think that's why Aaron's so hard right now. He likes that this is deviant. That he's violating the rules and me at the same time.

He grips onto the cable ties around my wrists, which are bound behind my back. He pushes me down so that my chest lies flat on the mattress as he fucks me. The cable ties are too tight, but he obviously intended for them to be since my encouragement to keep them loose didn't seem to register when he was putting them on. This is his way, and I haven't discouraged it because I don't want to scare him off. I need him if I want to be close to Brad.

He leans down and licks behind my ear. As his saliva taints my flesh, I feel disgusting for what I'm doing. That I'm letting him use and abuse me like this. That I'm about to be filled with him because of my obsession with someone who's been a dick to me ever since our first sexual encounter.

His cock burns inside me because of his less-than-generous use of lube. I think about how I wish I could shake off my feelings for Brad. It's too late for me, though. I've never felt this sort of burning passion before. Never felt anything that life-giving. Anything that made me feel as if, for a moment, all the worries and stresses I'd ever felt had vanished and been replaced with just that moment. Brad freed me, and I need that again. I need to feel that ease. And if I can't get it through Brad, I don't know if I'll ever feel that way again.

I feel the push that lets me know Aaron is coming. He collapses on top of me. Panting. Grunting. The rank scent of his sweat hits my nostrils like the stench of garbage.

After we clean up and get dressed, he guides me back downstairs, carefully playing lookout to make sure no one catches my escape. We enter a study with an oval table that seats over a dozen chairs. Guiding me to the window that I snuck in through, I open it. As I'm about to climb through, he snatches my wrist and pulls me to him. He forces a kiss, reminding me that there's no chemistry between us. I wonder how *he* feels. Is there some spark that he thinks is between us? Or does he get off knowing that I'm not into it? That he thinks I'm just using him to get into Alpha Theta Mu?

A click. Sounds like someone coming in.

"Shit," Aaron mutters.

I duck down.

"Hey!" Aaron calls.

"Hey, man." Brad's voice is a sweet melody as it hits my ears. "I went ahead and rounded everyone up so we could go over a few things before the meeting. I tried to text you, but I—"

"Great," Aaron says.

I crawl under the table. I can hide here until everyone clears out.

The guys shuffle in and take seats. I recognize Brad's boat shoes and his light strands of leg hair from the orientation. He stands behind a chair.

"Tonight's really important for us," he says. "Considering the incident we had last year, we can't afford to take on any pledges who might have questionable pasts."

A brothers hanged himself in his dormitory during one of the fraternity's spring formals. When the autopsy revealed various injuries across his body, the media had a field day. Though the injuries were concerning, the medical examiner determined that the death was a suicide. That didn't keep the press from making accusations of foul play, though. Or claiming that potentially excessive hazing had led the guy, who had a history of suicidal ideation, to taking his own life. That in mind, it makes sense that they're concerned about their new pledges.

"I don't want to bring this up around the brothers," Brad continues, "because I don't want to keep opening old wounds, but I think we should do our best to discourage the others from choosing guys who could potentially be problematic. Anyone who has any previous history of serious mental illness."

"Agreed," Aaron says as he takes a seat behind me. "Vice Archon and I have pulled out a few who we've noticed have seemed more problematic than the rest. We've done some background checks."

"Can you do that?" I recognize Tad's voice. He sounds baffled. Amused, even. Like he's waiting for Aaron to admit he's just kidding.

If they ran one on me, I'm fucked. But if that was the case, I wouldn't be here right now. Aaron would have found a way to get me out of here or convinced them to take the meeting somewhere else. And why would he need to check me out when he liked me? I'm suddenly relieved that I've been fucking him all this time.

"We did what we had to do," Aaron says. "We're not taking any risks this year. We want to make sure we know about any concerning psychological histories or even criminal records. It's something we should have already been doing. If we had, we wouldn't have pledged Keegan Rafferty and gotten all that heat last year over something that had nothing to do with us."

"But this isn't exactly on the level," Tad says.

"We have to protect Alpha Theta Mu. Rayden University doesn't give a shit about if we make it through this year or not, and with the scrutiny that's going to be on us, we need to make sure that we do everything we can to ensure that this is a good PR year for us. So we all need to agree that we don't need to give the university a reason to fuck us over. This is something that has to be done. Does anyone disagree with that?"

Their silence suggests their agreement.

"Brad will review these names, and tonight we will find polite ways of dismissing any of the ones who have dubious pasts. We've already decided how each one will be objected to. If anyone wants to drop this idea altogether, and put Alpha Theta Mu at risk, you should speak up now."

No objections. Strange to think that Aaron knows I'm down here and isn't worried about saying this in front of me. I guess I don't have to worry about pledging. There's no way he'd be willing to let me in on something like this unless he trusted me. If he really trusts me, though, I feel terrible because I'm not here for him.

Brad settles in the chair opposite of Aaron and reviews some of the names, presumably from a file or folder. It's unsettling to think they've been digging around in our pasts. What if Aaron looked into mine? What if he's just keeping it from the other guys? But if he had, he would have brought it up. I doubt anyone could look into my past without becoming seriously concerned about my mental wellbeing.

I crawl and sit before Brad's feet, as if I'm his pet dog. I want him. So bad. I gaze at his shorts, imagining how nice it would be to yank them down and suck him off.

A greedy impulse stirs within me. I can't help myself. I stroke my hand down his leg.

He silences midsentence.

I didn't think that through. If he says anything—if he so much as thinks this is some sort of gag and tries to discover the source of the touch—I won't wind up pledging for sure. Aaron won't be able to protect me once they discover he's broken the rules. Thinking quickly of a way to let him know it's me, I tuck my face against his leg the way I tucked my face against his chest after we fucked that first time. It's a gentle nudge. Something I'm not even sure he'll pick up on. But I hope it's enough.

He coughs and continues reading through his information about one of the prospective pledges.

BRAD

What the fuck is he doing?

While I reviewed the list of guys Aaron and I added to our shit-list last night, I felt something on my leg. The stroke of a hand. My gut instinct told me it was a prank. I acted calm because if the guys saw me freak, they'd get a good laugh out of it. And I wasn't going to give them the goddamn satisfaction. Then I felt something familiar—something that assured me it wasn't a prank. I remembered it all too well from when Ian curled up against me and tucked his face against my chest after we fucked in my orientation adviser's office. We lay on the desk together when he did it. It wasn't the way a guy touches someone he just wants to fuck. It was affectionate. What I hated even more about it is how much I wanted him to touch me like that.

I look at Aaron. I'm pissed. He's broken the rules, and he's broken it with my Ian, who whether I like it or not is definitely getting through tonight. I tried to fight it. Aaron hasn't understood my issue from the get-go. When he asked about my first slight against him, I said I thought Ian was a privileged asshole. But my opinion doesn't match the other brothers' feelings. Everyone likes him. He's sociable. Fun. I hoped that when Aaron mentioned background checks, we'd get one on him and find something that would prevent his entry, but Aaron refused. I did one on my own, though, and after what I discovered, I know if we'd gone that route, Ian would've been blackballed for sure. I've considered blowing his cover. Telling Aaron what I've discovered. But if I did, Aaron would start to wonder about my obsession with his new boy-toy.

It would've been so much easier if I could have blackballed him, but I have to accept that I have to find a way to bear being around him for the rest of the year. And unfortunately, despite my frustration, I'm thrilled about it.

He massages my crotch, and I know my stiffening erection will only encourage him. I'd feel bad about betraying Aaron if it wasn't his goddamn fault that I'm in this mess to begin with. I considered telling him about orientation when I was urging him to get a background check on Ian, but it was too late for the reveal. I'd come too far to start dishing out the truth.

Ian undoes the button on my shorts and unzips them. His movements are slow enough that he doesn't make any noise, and I raise my voice as I review the prospective pledges to keep anyone from hearing any unintended sounds he might make.

A rush of confidence sweeps through me.

I won't deny Ian this. Because I want it too much. If I get just another taste, maybe I'll see that it isn't as incredible as I thought it was before.

But what if the guys catch on? Surely, I can't make it through this meeting without anyone figuring out what's up. Especially if Aaron is right across from us.

I lift my ass up as Ian slides my shorts and briefs down to my ankles.

Between the excitement of having this opportunity and the adrenaline from knowing how easily we could get caught, my dick is painfully hard. So hard I wish I could just rub one out before letting Ian do anything because I'm liable to blow any second now.

I feel warm lips around my dick. He wets it, lubing it up before pulling back, leaving me in unbearable suspense. As I continue reading, I reach under the table for his hair. I want to snatch it and force him back onto my cock, but when I don't feel him, I give up because anymore effort will give me away.

I wait impatiently for him to offer something. Anything. He's teasing me. Playing with my mind. Punishing me for ignoring him. For fucking his best friend. He has every right to hurt me like this, but all I want to do is stop this meeting and fuck the shit out of him.

I feel his hand grip my shaft and stroke up and down.

Sweat starts down my forehead.

I wipe it off as I continue discussing the particular pledge I'm on, trying to seem competent because if Aaron catches on, I'm a dead man.

Ripples of sensation race up my pelvis, exciting me further, and as I feel Ian's mouth join his hand's work, I feel for his hair and grip onto it. He's not getting away again. If this is the only chance I have with him, I'm taking it.

He works with what little range he has, compensating with skillful licks. Teasing the head. Sliding up and down the shaft.

I feel my come working its way from my balls through my shaft. The tension it creates forces me to rock my pelvis to help it on its way.

I wipe away some more sweat on my forehead before I move on to the next sheet with details about the potentials we're dismissing. I feel I appear even more competent than usual because I'm working so hard to keep anyone from discovering the ruse.

I look directly into Aaron's eyes. He has a smug look on his face. Like he knows he's getting away with something. I can't help but delight in this even more. Knowing that Ian is still mine. The appreciation is bittersweet because I'm not eager to betray my brother. Not after everything Aaron has done for me. And he's done more than I could ever repay him for.

I can stop this at any time. All I have to do is pull him away, but I won't.

As I feel myself climaxing, I want to jerk about wildly and unleash all the passion that builds within me, but I have to show as little as possible. I grip tighter onto the folder with one hand and onto Ian's hair with the other as I explode into his mouth.

"Fuck...fuck...I just lost where I'm at," I say.

I cling to his hair, holding his head in place.

As I regroup and continue reading, I release him. He pulls his mouth back, and his tongue runs across the head of my dick. My cock's so hypersensitive. I want to grab him by the hair and force him away, but he spends his time there, trying to get all my come into his mouth.

Such a good fucking bottom. He could be mine, but he can't be. And that makes the experience I just allowed myself to have even worse.

The fleeting moment of passion and ecstasy devolves into guilt and shame.

Whatever game Ian and me are playing, I'm losing.

4

IAN

I can't see, but the hum of the car I'm in the backseat of is as soothing as the thick scent that fills the air.

It's my second week as a pledge. Jesse and I have already endured a few of Alpha Theta Mu's rituals. In one instance, the guys locked a bunch of us in a room and made us listen to music with the volume amped up. In another, we were forced to strip to our boxers and raid the Phi Theta sorority down the street. I can only imagine what this latest adventure will entail. Earlier tonight, my big brother Tad called to let me know Jesse and I needed to wait for some of the brothers to arrive at our place. They would take us to our next location for the rest of the ritual. Lawrence and Tad showed up to our apartment, tied us up, and blindfolded us. They put me in the back of a car, and I'm guessing they took Jesse to another because the only sounds I've heard since I've been in here have come from the driver's seat.

I recognize the aroma that fills the car from having my face buried in Brad's cock.

He must've signed up to take me to the next location. I want to believe it's because he wanted to get me alone. Considering what he let me do to him on bid day, I know he still wants me. But since pledging Alpha Theta Mu, I haven't had a chance to get him alone. To let him know how much I want him. How much I need him. He's avoided me at every event. At every meeting he doesn't even look at me. Surely because he feels like he's betrayed Aaron. But that's not doing me any favors.

Before Brad, every day was painful. Every day my chest constricted and my muscles locked with tension. My thoughts ran through various scenarios—played out the many ways I could free myself from the crippling sensations that, at times, made it hard to get out of bed. Sometimes the thoughts come so quickly that it's hard to escape a public moment—sneak off to the restroom or to some equally private location—to collapse to the floor, shivering as the dark thoughts overtake me. They aren't thoughts that seem to originate within me. They're a thousand voices shouting at me. They are the living nightmare I've endured for so long. Pain quiets the voices. Or at least dulls my awareness of them. Pinching my arm. Bashing my fist into my leg. Such temporary relief. But more effective than any therapist's well-intentioned words. Or pills that have only scattered my mind, making the voices come and go in a way that was even more concerning than when they were a constant threat. When Brad fucked me, though, throughout that experience, the pain he put me through silenced all the voices. Silenced all the hate I have for myself. In that moment, I experienced a high far beyond anything I'd encountered before. My emotions ceased their assault on my consciousness. And that's where I want to get to again. That's why I need this so much.

Brad wants me, and I want him. That should be enough. I'd just chosen Aaron because I thought it would get me closer to Brad, but now that I understand their friendship, I realize why that's such a shitty idea. I could have chosen any other brother in the house and it wouldn't have been a big deal. But because it's Aaron, I'm off-limits.

This is my chance to get Brad again, though. Or at least to know if it's worth the effort. If he can push me away, then I must be wrong about how he feels. This is my chance to find out if I've been lying to myself all this time. If I should just give up. Or maybe if we do something and it isn't as hot, I'll be free of this horrible pain within me.

BRAD

Stupidest idea ever.

I shouldn't have volunteered to pick him up, but since I know how rough some of the guys can get during the rituals, I wasn't about to let some other asshole manhandle Ian. And I knew Aaron wouldn't volunteer because he didn't want to appear biased toward him. Just like I didn't want to seem biased toward Jesse. So I stepped up to the plate. I could tell Aaron was relieved it was me, but if he understood why I really volunteered, he would've been concerned about his trick.

"You can fuck me if you want," Ian says.

My muscles tense up like they would if someone was insulting me. "How the fuck did you know it was me?"

"I can smell you."

His words creep me out, but also arouse me.

"I was just letting you know," he continues, "that if you wanted to pull over and fuck me, I wouldn't stop you."

My dick is so fucking hard right now.

God-fucking-damn him. As if every day since he's pledged I haven't thought about taking his hole. As if I haven't conspired to find a way of getting him alone and tricking him into fucking me again. As a brother and Vice Archon, I have so much control over him. But I've been wise enough not to abuse my power the way I've so desperately wanted to abuse him. It doesn't stop me from imagining twisted scenarios where I rough him up. Show him how much I want to tear him apart. Fortunately, I have Jesse to help me unleash some of those fantasies on. It's not enough, and being with the real thing only makes me feel like I've been missing out on something that I don't want to die without having ever experienced again.

I just have to get to the rendezvous point, which is only a few miles away. It's an abandoned warehouse, where we'll strip the guys down and make them wrestle in a kiddie pool of mud until there's a victor.

It'd be easy to claim I got lost. I could have accidentally put the wrong address into my phone. Could have made an innocent mistake of driving Ian to the last place where we performed our Alpha Theta Mu ritual. Things like that happen all the time. I've heard plenty of excuses that give me every reason to stop right here and give Ian what we both want.

"You know we're not supposed to talk," I say. "So keep that up and I'll report you. Then you'll be really fucked, okay?"

"Jesse tells me about what you guys do, and I know you need more than that."

Saliva rushes into my mouth as though I've seen a delicious meal after having gone a day without eating.

"Just stop," I say.

"You can do whatever you want to me."

I pull over on the side of the road and turn to him.

"I told you, I can't do that."

"You didn't have a problem before."

"That day in the study was a mistake. I didn't even know who you were."

"Bullshit."

His face is locked in a stiff expression. I can tell that a small part of him is scared that I'm being honest, and I won't make him believe that he is meaningless to me. I'm not that heartless.

"No, I knew. And I knew it was wrong too. We made a mistake. But on top of me being the worst thing that could ever happen to you, now you're screwing my best friend, and I'm not going to do anything else behind his back."

"Like he doesn't do anything behind *my* back?"

A fair point since Aaron has at least four different pledges he's fucking. However, as far as Aaron's concerned, Ian is his property. He doesn't share his toys. Never has.

"Just come back here," Ian says. "Talk to me."

Temptress!

He doesn't want to talk. He knows what will happen if I get back there.

"Fuck you." I say it because I hate that he can control me like this. That he knows how much I want him. How much I ache for him. How much I need him. I hate that he knows that all I want to do is take him out into the woods beside us and fuck him until he bleeds. It's this demon within me. This passion that, when he's around, is too much for me. I've even had to leave the room when he's there because I know that I'll try to do something. My body isn't my own right now. I can tell when I try to move too close to him, and when I accidently end up beside him. Or in this case, when I've put myself in the position to be alone with him.

He springs from the back and kisses before him, missing my lips but hitting my cheek. He kisses across to my lips.

The fire that surges through me is too much for me to deny. I take the kiss, feeling his soft lips on mine. Appreciating them. Loving them. Why does he have to feel so good? I despise Aaron because all I can think is how I wish this was mine. However, considering this darkness within me and Ian's evident suicidal nature, I know how dangerous it is. But in this moment, what's right evaporates. I shove him back against the seat and climb over the console. His hands are still bound behind him, and as much as I feel I should free him before we go any further, I can't help myself. I need to be inside him. Filling him. Feeling his dry hole.

I lift his legs and pull his shoes off. Then I undo his pants and pull them up with his briefs. Soon, I have my own jeans and underwear at my knees. After I offer myself a few spits for lube, I stab into him. He cringes as he opens his mouth wide and screams so loud that if anyone was within thirty yards of the car, I'm sure they hear him. I'm not gentle. I know what he wants. And maybe if I'm rough enough, he'll learn that it isn't what he wants. That it shouldn't be what anyone wants.

As he screams out, I ram into him, my cock pushing into his unwilling hole.

He twists, struggling but not refusing my intrusions.

I remove his blindfold. I want him to see me take him. I want him to see my desire.

I should stop. I regret every thrust. I regret how I cling to his legs as I push in deeper and deeper. A tear rushes down his cheek, and I can tell it's too much for him, but he begs, "Harder!"

So I obey.

It's not enough, though. I pull out, and he gazes at me with a desperate expression. I flip him over and press him down on his chest so that he's stretched out across the seat. I yank his jeans the rest of the way down and toss them on the floor with his briefs before spreading his legs. Ducking and maneuvering, I slide into him from behind, shoving so quickly that he cries out as loudly as he did the first time I pushed within him. I wrap my arm around his throat and pull back so that he's in a surely wildly uncomfortable position—one he doesn't complain about. But I like knowing how much it hurts him, and I can tell by the way he grunts he likes it too.

He's so tight.

I bite at his neck. Softly at first. Then I take a much harder bite that makes him moan.

"You're my bitch," I say. "You're mine. You're fucking mine."

What am I saying? Why am I doing this?

"Yes, I am," he says. "I'm all yours."

His words of reassurance make me feel that same lack of inhibition that I felt that first time we fucked.

I grip his hair and shove his face into the seat cushion. With my other hand, I grab his bound wrists and pull them up, straining them.

He cries out.

"Is this what you wanted from me?"

As I raise them higher, he screams even louder.

I restrain myself. I want to hurt him like he needs to be hurt, but no more. Nothing that could seriously injure this beautiful boy.

I raise his arms some more, drilling within him as it becomes easier and easier to insert myself.

"Fuck, fuck, fuck," he says.

I pull out and urge him onto his back. I slide his shirt up and pull the collar over his head, tucking it behind his neck. Then I remove my shirt before I pull his legs apart and reenter him. I spit across his body just to claim him. I can tell by the way he rolls his eyes back that he's loving it. I lean down, and as he opens his mouth, I grab his face and force him close as I spit directly into his mouth. He swallows it quickly, and I offer him another. When he opens his mouth for me to offer it again, I spit on his face instead to remind him that he doesn't get to decide what I give him.

He leans forward like he wants a kiss, but instead, I grab his head and cock it back so that he can't see me. So that he knows that I control what he gets to see. With my other hand, I squeeze his erect cock. Then I reach down to his balls while I'm pushing within him and grip on tight.

"Oh, shit," he says as he squirms.

"Uh uh. Be good."

He stills, though it's clear that his body is encouraging him to move. To fight against me.

"You're mine," I say again, though I don't know what's possessing me to say this because I know he's not and that I can't do this. But as I'm inside him, taking him, a primal force controls me. Makes me want to break him. Makes me want to hurt him so that he truly understands the meaning of the word *pain*.

I squeeze his balls even tighter.

He curses, and I release them and clasp onto his throat with both hands. I grip so tight that his face turns pink.

I wonder about the pressure on his arms as they're bound behind him, pinned beneath his body. He seems fine, though. As he struggles to breathe, a rush of adrenaline soars through me. His breath and his life are totally within my control. He depends on me. He needs me. He trusts me in a way that he shouldn't.

I release him and grip onto his thighs as I continue fucking him.

He cries out, "Hit me."

I know that's what he wants. I've known it since that first encounter. I slap him so hard that his head jerks to the side, leaving a pink mark illuminated from the streetlamp that beams in through the window. He recovers and looks at me defiantly. It's as if he's challenging me to strike him even harder. As if I've disappointed him for not making it hurt more. I consider what I learned about him in the background check. The dark secrets he hasn't shared with me. The things that are surely part of the reason why he's like this. And I understand why he needs the relief.

I give him another slap and lean down to him, staring into his eyes to let him know who is in charge.

Although, I know it's him.

His breath slaps against my face as I force within him again and again. I can tell he's in more pain than he's willing to show me. So I grab his nipple and twist sharply. He'll show me his pain whether he likes it or not. He growls, but doesn't let up his gaze.

I grip onto his chin and insert my thumb into his mouth. He sucks on it like he's trying to let me know just how much he wants to please me. How much he wants my body.

I'm getting so fucking close.

He maintains eye contact. I'm about to blow.

I pull back to get out of him, but he wraps his legs around me.

Devious bastard.

I give him another good slap, one that makes him curse, but he maintains his hold to my waist. I struggle against him, pulling out just in time as my come oozes from the head of my dick. I stroke my cock as it spews onto the rim of his asshole.

That's all you get, you greedy whore.

He looks to me with sad eyes. I can tell he knows I've filled Jesse, and he's jealous. That just makes me want him even more.

I like knowing that I can hurt him like this, especially considering all the grief he's given me since the first day we met.

I shift my cock about so that the head runs in a circle around his hole as I collect the semen around it before shoving my dick back inside.

"Untie me so that I can jerk off," he says.

"No."

"What?" His expression sobers.

I snatch his cock and stroke it myself. His pleasure is mine. His load is mine. I get to choose when he releases it. I pound him as hard as I did before, my cock springing back to life. It's an impressive display of my refractory period.

I lean down, stroking my thumb across the head of his dick.

"I want you to come for me. Come all over yourself."

He whimpers before releasing himself across the back of my thumb. He keeps coming and coming, reminding me that he has a big-ass load.

I pull back to witness his explosion as he continues shooting across himself. As he releases his last bit across his abs, I collect it in my hand and pull it to my face. I lick it up and swish it around in my mouth.

He watches like he doesn't know how to respond.

I lean down—still inside him—and get right before his face.

He must sense what I want to do because he opens his mouth. I open mine, but I don't spit. Just allow the come to fall within his mouth.

It's disgusting. Vile. This boy will do anything I want him to. The fucking moron. Everything about how stupid he is— how moronic he is for wanting me the way he does—makes me want to show him that he needs to rethink these horrible priorities that are in his head. He's going to get hurt like this.

As he swallows his own seed, all I can do is kiss him because I'm terrified that it might be the last time we share this passion.

It has to be.

IAN

I wasn't eager to swallow my own come, but I'll do anything he wants. Anything so he won't let me go again. Anything so he'll admit that this is right. If this experience hasn't shown him that the passion between us is too strong to deny, I don't know what will.

He lay on top of me, catching his breath from the effort he put into our workout. My gaze settles on the mole on his cheek—a beauty make that has always appeared to me to be the symbolic signature of the artist who crafted this beautiful specimen.

My legs hurt from the awkward positions he forced me into. My ass feels as if someone's driven nails into it. My arms are the only thing that seem to have been spared pain since lying on them has put them to sleep.

He's done a good number on me, but I don't have any complaints because even when it hurt it felt good. He shifts about and pushes himself up onto his palms. As his gaze wanders, I know what he's thinking. He regrets what we've done. I hate him for that because our moments together are the only thing that give me the relief I've needed for so long. Too many times I've dreamt about how wonderful it would be to just end it all. To finally defeat this burning pain within me. But with Brad, that all goes away, and it terrifies me to think that he'll deny me the only thing that's ever offered me freedom from that hurt.

"What's wrong?" I ask. Not that I need to.

"We can't do this."

"Oh my God. Just cut it with that shit, will you?"

"No. This isn't right. What we do...it's..."

"Hot," I say. I lean up for a kiss.

He pushes me down.

"I can't do this," he says.

A sharp pain stirs in my chest, nearly as acute as the pain in my ass. He crawls to the other side of the car, where he fetches his boxers and jeans and squirms into them.

I sit up. Lifting my ass, I slide my wrists under and down my legs until my hands are before me. I scoot close to him and grip onto his beefy arm.

"Why not?" I ask.

"You're reckless. You obviously don't have any concern about getting hurt."

"I would stop you if I thought you were going to really hurt me."

"Would you?" he asks.

"Of course I would. What the fuck is this about?"

He stares at me like he's considering sharing the truth, but I can tell he won't.

"I deserve a reason."

"You don't deserve anything. We shouldn't have done this. Aaron's gonna be—"

"I don't give a fuck about Aaron, and you know that. And what about Jesse?"

"Jesse knows what we are."

"And Aaron couldn't care less if I was any of the other guys he was fucking. I'm not his property."

"You're more his property than you realize."

I want to punch him, but instead, I feel tears stirring in my eyes. I slide across the seat to get away from him.

"I'm not the one trying to pretend like there's nothing here," I say.

"I'm not pretending anything. I'm telling you that nothing can come of it. Do you understand that? I'm not going to change my mind. So you can keep pushing, but at the end of the day, you're going to have to get over the fact that nothing can happen between us."

The tears are sliding quickly down my cheeks. Not because I have any romantic feelings for this prick. Just because, in this moment, I hate his guts for depriving me of what I really want. His body. His touch. His kiss. His abuse.

That hit he offered that first time we were together and the ones he gave me this time are the only things that have satisfied this hunger within me. My dom two years ago couldn't fill this need like he can. It's why I haven't picked that BDSM shit back up. It never satisfied me. I thought it could, but the control...the rules...the role-play wasn't enough. I needed more than a hit or a slap. At the time, I didn't know what that was. I didn't realize it until my encounter with Brad—that first time when the passion ignited within me and he soothed something deep within. It wasn't just the act that I craved. It was his passion behind it. The need in him to do that to me. And when I experienced it for the first time, it was as if I'd come up for air after having my head held under water to the point of nearly drowning.

"Don't do this to me," I say. I'm not above begging.

As he looks to me, I see the concern in his eyes. He cares. He doesn't want to leave me in this desperate state.

"I can do whatever to make you feel like it's safer."

He shakes his head.

"I've hurt someone like this," he says, his gaze shifting quickly. "Badly. And I've learned that I just can't control myself. Not the way I need to. Even with this, it got so much worse than I'd hoped. I thought maybe I could control it, but I can't. There's something about you, Ian. Something that makes me want to tear you apart. Can't you see how wrong that is? Can't you see how fucked up I have to be to want that?"

"But I want it too."

"That's what scares me."

He quiets. Stares forward, lost in thought.

The guys are going to wonder where we are. They're probably blowing up his phone right now. But I'm not going to mention it to him because I don't want this moment to end. Painful as it is, I'll take this over not being near him.

"When we ran the background checks on some of the other guys," he says. "I ran one on you too. Behind Aaron's back."

I freeze. Some things I can't escape.

"I know about that pedophile," he continues.

My hurt transforms into rage.

"You don't know shit," I say.

I'm still crying, and it's even worse now that he's brought back one of the most painful experiences of my life.

I grab my briefs off the floor and hurry out the door. With my wrists still bound together, I scurry into my briefs and start down the road. I pull my shirt collar back over my head and tug my shirt down until it covers my nude torso. I don't know where the fuck I'm going to go looking like this, but I can't be around him. Not right now.

"Ian! Ian!"

He dashes out of the car and chases after me. He grabs my arm and pulls me back.

I yank away from him. Clasping my hands together, I pound against him. I know I can't do much damage to his powerful body, but any sting is enough for me.

"Leave me alone, you fucking asshole!"

He snatches my wrists. I continue struggling, but he doesn't let go.

"Ian, please! Stop!"

I surrender as I lose what strength I have left. I burst into tears and lean against him, using his nude chest to hide my face.

"You didn't do anything wrong," he assures me. "It's not your fucking fault. You were just a kid and he took advantage of you."

I pull away again. "He didn't do anything to me that I didn't want him to do."

"You were sixteen."

"Sixteen's legal in Georgia, you dumbass. It was only illegal because he was a teacher."

"And what about the whips, handcuffs..."

"It's called BDSM, and he sure as hell was a lot safer than anything you guys are into."

Silence.

"I didn't mean it like that."

"Yes, you did."

"No. That's what I didn't like about it. It was too safe. I was going to call it off before his wife found out and reported him. Before that bitch got video of us—"

"How could you want him to do that to you?"

"You didn't pick that up in the background check? Did the trail of therapists and psychologists throw you off?" I'm practically screaming at him because he didn't have a right to look into my past. To know about the things he must've discovered.

He doesn't say anything, but I can tell by the look in his eyes that he knows what I'm referring to.

"I've had the best therapists money can buy, and they can't make it better."

"You were a kid. It was an accident."

"How the fuck do you accidentally shoot your brother?"

Tears fill my eyes as I recall Jacob on the floor, motionless. So different from the kid I was used to seeing. Always smiling. Always laughing. Blood rushed down his forehead, moving toward his lifeless blue eyes—eyes that used to sparkle as we bounced around the living room with our Power Ranger action figures.

I wonder what Brad's thinking. Is he judging me? Is he pitying me?

"Ian, I—"

"I don't need your sympathy. I just need you to fuck me."

I need him right now. After everything he's stirred up, I ache. I hunger. I pine.

"We're seriously fucked up," he says. "We need therapy. Not to be seeing each other."

He starts to head back to the car, but I grab his arm and pull him back to me, pushing up against him. I kiss him passionately, reminding him of why he has to give me a chance. He surrenders, which makes the kiss even more gratifying. Once again, his kiss erases everything we just discussed. Wipes it from my mind.

I'm free.

My dick hardens. He pushes away from me.

"Come on, Ian. We can't fucking do it."

"You're not doing either of us any favors by stopping this. I'm not asking for anything other than sex. Please. Just fuck me. Fuck me like you want to fuck me. I won't ask for a commitment. You know why I need this. Just give it to me. Make it hurt. Make me cry."

He looks at me the way I imagine he would look at a panhandler. With pity and disgust. But I'm not ashamed of what I want.

"You're a fucking masochist," he says.

"And you're a sadist. Doesn't that make us perfect for each other?"

He lunges at me, kissing me again. An explosion of energy chases all my thoughts away. I hope he's as caught up in these sensations as I am, so he won't stop this next encounter.

Take me, Brad. Hurt me. Break me.

5

BRAD

"Fuck, fuck, yeah. Fuck me," Ian whispers against my face as I assault him with kisses.

"Keep quiet," I say.

I don't want anyone at the Lambda Phi mixer going on right outside the bathroom to hear what we're up to.

I'm inside him, my arms wrapped under his thighs as I fuck him against the wall. I can tell by the way he cringes that he's in serious pain, but I drive in even harder. The look he gives me—one of desire and lust—assures me that I'm giving it to him the way he wants it.

He reminds me of Keegan. How eager he was. How he wanted it to hurt. He wanted everything I had to give, but now that I know what that can lead to, I have to be careful.

Ian knows I'm holding back. I see the longing for more in his eyes every time we sneak away. When we fuck in my car. Or in the bathroom stalls at the fitness center on campus. Or on the rare occasion when he sneaks out of Aaron's room and comes to mine. I cherish those nights most because when he's in my room, I can pretend, at least for a little while, that he's mine. Just mine.

Why did I agree to this? But I know why. I can't keep running from him. I fell right into his trap, but it's the only trap I want to be caught in. The part that stings is that we're doing it behind Aaron's back. Aaron and me don't keep secrets. Not like this. We're open with each other, and considering what he's done for me—how much trouble he's saved me from—this seems to me the most ungrateful of acts. I owe him more than I could ever repay him for. But that hasn't stopped me from betraying him.

I shouldn't care as much as I do. He's inviting plenty of pledges back to his room. Not giving any more shits about Ian than any of the others. We shouldn't have to do this. I shouldn't have to see the marks that he leaves on Ian's body. All his wounds should be inflicted by me. But it's my fault for insisting that we continue with things as they are. That's the best way to keep Aaron from becoming suspicious.

I bite down on Ian's neck. I like knowing that our buddies are all out there, unaware of the secrets we keep in the bathroom at Lambda Phi's house.

Sensation wells in my cock, and I feel this powerful energy forcing me to thrust in him.

The past few times we've hooked up, I haven't gone too far, but I can feel this darkness within me—this maniac waiting to unleash so much pain on him. Waiting to injure him beyond repair. It's my own Mr. Hyde. It wants to destroy. To humiliate. To defile.

I know where it comes from. It's hard for me to separate intimacy from those nights when my mom would sneak into my bedroom and cuddle with me. Her breath would smell of chardonnay as she stroked my body a little too much. Offered a few too many kisses. "Show me that you love me," she would say, and when it was a struggle for me to satisfy her, she would become enraged. She would hit and slap in places she knew she wouldn't leave marks for Dad to see.

I first started having the fits at school. I would be listening to the lecture one moment and thrashing about the next. My teachers insisted on therapy, but Dad wouldn't have anyone suggesting one of his own was mentally ill, so he paid the right people through every fit and every fight these fits caused through high school. But what he never understood—what no one understood—was that whatever rage took over my body in those moments was beyond my control. And that terrified the shit out of me. It was only during my first sexual encounters that I learned I could tame the violent spirit by offering it what it really wanted: someone else's pain. It's what led me to someone like Keegan. And it's what led me to someone like Ian.

I pull out of him and lower him. He continues kissing me until I push him from me and turn him around. I press his chest against the wall and shove back within him from behind. He claws at the wall as I thrust forcefully within him. He turns, and I can tell by the way he's opening his mouth that he wants to scream out.

He takes a breath and whispers, "Please come in me."

In all the times we've hooked up, it's something I've avoided because it would be like me claiming ownership of him. And he's not mine. He's Aaron's.

"That's not happening," I whisper.

He's tried to make me come in him a few times, wrapping his legs around my leg at just the right moments, and he must know by now that I'm not so easily fooled.

"Please," he begs again.

"Just shut the fuck up."

"Fill me. I need it. I really do," he says, turning to me so that I can see a tear shifting in his eye.

His pleading like this just makes it even more difficult for me. Makes my dick stiff like a rock.

I push him forward so that his dick is pressed between his pelvis and the wall. I can tell by what little noise he allows to escape through his lips that he's in pain. I love it because the beast is quiet. Because the act satisfies its hunger.

I grab at his side. Tugging at it. Grinding my fingers against him. Trying to leave marks. To taint his body. It feels so good. So right.

I grip onto his face and shove my fingers in his mouth. He arches his back sharply as I twist his head so that he has to look me in the eyes.

"You're mine," I say again.

I hate myself every time I say it. I might as well be telling him I love him, which I sure as fuck don't. It's just this goddamn inexplicable chemistry that I wish I could escape. As I gaze into his eyes, I feel like I'm about to come. I pull back.

He wraps his leg behind him, clinging on to my leg so that I can't escape.

"No, no," I cry out.

He doesn't let go, and I don't really want him to.

I knew it would happen. I could have pulled out sooner. But I wanted to breed him. I wanted to possess him, and it's so fucking satisfying.

He jerks off his own cock. I grab his hair and yank on it as his eyes roll back while he shoots onto the wall. Panting together, we fall from our high. I pull out of him, spin him around, and kiss him passionately. Until my lips are numb. No matter how much of him I taste, it's never enough. Pushing him back to the wall, we pull away from each other briefly. We breathe against each other's faces. As I look into his eyes, I know that he has me totally under his spell. He's magic. A vision. And I'm the monster who wants to destroy him.

I won't hurt him. Not like Keegan. That was different. There was a reason I was so fucking pissed.

But it still showed that this rage could get beyond my control, and I can't ever let it go that far.

I kiss him again, igniting that familiar, sweet passion that I always feel with him.

AARON

Little shit.

I'm going to find out what he's been up to.

I've seen the wounds that he gets from whoever he's fucking behind my back. We're not exclusive, but I'm not used to a guy like Ian. My other pledges push for something more. At least try to couple up. They want the power they think they'll get by being associated with the Archon. Not Ian, though. He's different. He doesn't seem to give a fuck about how I could benefit him. His disinterest isn't something I'm used to. I imagine it's because I can't quench his thirst for pain. Brad insisted I run a background check on him, but I refused since I'd already run one and discovered Ian's colorful history with a dom. The teacher he fucked was charged for sexual assault, but Daddy's investigator assured me that the case files show that Ian considered the relationship consensual. A guy with a dom at sixteen is far more experienced than these other pledges. I do my best to fulfill his desires. Use a little less lube. Slap him that much harder. Fuck him in the most uncomfortable positions I can imagine. The new injuries he's received—ones he blames on the Thursday Alpha Theta Mu flag football games—have convinced me that he needs it rougher than I've given it to him. The marks on his side today, obviously fingerprints, assured me that he hooked up with whoever it was again. When I noticed them, he tried to blame them on me, but I know where I mark my bitches.

"Hey, man, what's up?" Brad asks as he enters my room.

I rise from my desk and approach him. I texted him a few minutes earlier to meet me in here. "Not much. Just trying to organize next week's mixer with Theta Beta Phi."

I trust Brad more than the other guys. He owes me. Big time. He'll do whatever I ask. Plus, since he's hooking up with Ian's roommate, he has better access to the kid's secrets than anyone else.

I review some of the plans for the mixer, discussing possible budget cuts since Tad threw a fit when he saw how much Theta Beta Phi wanted to spend on the event. Considering how much he's increased our budget through his bookkeeping, we're eager to keep our Treasurer happy. Once we find a few odds and ends we can throw out—or at least, that Brad can sweet-talk Kelly at Theta Beta Phi into cutting out—I ease into my next request: "You mind if I ask you for a favor?"

"Anything." His serious expression coupled with his thoughtless agreement assure me he's the right person for the job.

"I think Ian's been running around on me."

"What makes you think that?"

"Just trust me on this. He's doing something with someone. I was going to see if you might keep an eye on him for me."

"What's the big deal? You have plenty of guys?"

"This one's serious. You're with Jesse all the time, so it'll be effortless for you. Just hang out around him when he's using his phone. See who he's texting. See if you can maybe get a hold of it."

"What difference does it make?"

It's a good question. Why should I fixate on him over the others? Is it just because he's the only one that isn't interested in taking advantage of my position? Or because I want to win him from whoever is satisfying his darker desires? The reason doesn't matter, though. Just that I've decided he's mine.

"Because if he is, then I want to just fucking end it."

Or find a way to scare this other asshole off my piece of ass. I have too much money and too many connections to have to worry about competition. Although, it wouldn't be the first time. The bitter reminder stirs my hatred toward Brad. The dumbass may be willing to bend over backwards to help me out of a jam, but I have nothing but contempt for him.

"Understand?" I ask.

"I'll keep an eye on him, man. But maybe if you feel like this, you should just call it off."

"I really like this guy. I just want to make sure I'm not barking up the wrong tree."

And by that, I mean I want to win. He's mine and only mine.

BRAD

"We can't do this anymore," I say.

"Why not?" Ian asks.

I met him at the pizza restaurant where he waits tables part-time. We've met here a few times since we started regularly fucking a few weeks earlier. He sits in the passenger's seat, looking adorable in his red visor, black polo, and khaki pants—the required uniform for his job. I want to take him right there, but I didn't come out here to fuck.

"Aaron's onto us," I say, knowing the best thing to do is just to get it out. "He asked me to keep an eye on you. See if you're messing around with someone."

"What business is that of his? Why am I supposed to be the good little boy when he's out doing whatever he wants?"

"It doesn't matter. You're officially off limits as long as he's put me on your tail."

"Well, while you're back there..."

I glare at him to let him know I'm not amused.

"You can't stop this," he says.

"Watch me."

He moves closer for a kiss. I recoil. He's surprised by my rejection, as he should be because up until now, I haven't had the strength.

"I'll just call it off with him," he says.

"And then when he sees me running around with you, you think he'll magically be totally cool and not suspicious at all? I should have known what a shitty idea this was. This is what happens when you betray a brother."

"Brad, this isn't fair to either of us. If we just talk to him—"

"I owe Aaron too much to let him know that I've done this to him."

"What could you possibly owe him?"

A silence fills the air as Ian's words stir the painful memories that I spend so much of my time trying to forget. Memories that I know I'll never forget.

"He was there for me last year. When I needed him. I owe him my loyalty. And it might suck, but I'm not going to be a dick to him."

"You'll just be a dick to me?"

This is hard enough as it is.

"He's done right by me, so I think it's fucking time I do the right thing."

I reflect on this pattern that I seem to be falling into. And I can't let it happen. Not again. Not after all Aaron has done for me.

"Brad—"

"You need to go."

His eyes water, as though he thinks this was all heading somewhere that it just wasn't.

"Don't be a bitch about it. This is life. Grow up and get the fuck out of here."

"Fuck you. You're such a coward. I fucking hate you."

His words stir a burning sensation in my chest, and even though I know he's being overdramatic, the thought of him hating me pains me.

He opens the door and hurries back into the restaurant.

I wait until he's inside before I bash my fists against the steering wheel and the console.

The monster within me awakens as I curse and shout out nonsense. The pain within me is so powerful, and the only relief I can find is in bashing my shoulder against the car door repeatedly.

IAN

"Pull over," Tad says. "I need to vomit."

One of the responsibilities we have as pledges is to play designated driver to the brothers, and since Tad is my big brother, I've had to play it a few times for him.

I pull the car over. He dashes out and hurries to the side of the road, where he hurls before the edge of the woods. I stand a few yards away, waiting patiently for him as he blows chunks a few more times. After he collects himself, I help him back into the car.

"God, I'm such a fucking mess," he says as I sit back in the driver's seat. "Remind me to stop by Finn's room to buy some oxycodone."

Finn interns at Emory Hospital and somehow manages to get away with swiping even the most regulated of meds to make some quick cash off the brothers—something they encourage as they race to him with their parents' cash. Not that the kid of a CPA and tax attorney can judge them for suckling at their parents' teats. I know I wouldn't be at Rayden without their support, but I try to take as little as possible, meaning I'm one of the few guys who's even bothered getting a part-time job.

Tad eyes me suspiciously as he settles. It's like he's trying to figure something out. "So you're seeing Brad too?"

"What?"

He leans his forehead against the window.

"I stole his phone the other day. Saw your texts about meeting up."

That dumbass didn't delete my texts? Seriously? I've been so paranoid about Jesse finding mine that they're in the trash about as soon as I get them.

I'm terrified about what Tad might have told Aaron.

"Don't worry. I'm not ratting you out. Just want to tell you to be careful."

"What?"

He turns back to me. Despite the seriousness of this conversation, his wavering gaze and drooping face make it hard to concentrate on what he's saying.

"Just take my advice. Brad can lose his shit. Like seriously. You haven't seen him when he gets mad, but it's happened a few times, and he totally wigs out. I'm talking beating the crap out of guys. We pledged together, and when one of the brothers called him a faggot, he beat the living shit out of him. I seriously thought the guy was going to report him to the cops."

"Well, I'm not going to call him a faggot, so I doubt—"

"Don't bullshit me. I know what he's into. And after what happened to Keegan… Let's just say the coroner may not have found anything, but Brad…he's got a temper on him."

"They were an item?"

He eyes me curiously. Like he's not sure if he should say more, but he doesn't have to. He's suggesting that Brad had something to do with Keegan's death. But he committed suicide. Although, I can't help but think about the injuries the medical examiner's office noted—the ones the press had a field day with. Surely those were from them fucking. But what if they weren't? What if there was more to it? What if Brad's dangerous? Tad seems to think he is.

"Keegan was his regular trick," Tad continues. "Look, Brad's a good guy, and I'm not saying that he *did* do anything. I'm not blabbing on him. Didn't say anything to the police. Not saying anything to you. But I know the way he is, and I'm just saying, there's a fine line between kinky and dangerous. You get me?"

"Yeah."

But I can't believe Tad. Brad's hurt me plenty since we started hooking up, but he wouldn't ever take things too far. Yet suddenly things make a lot more sense if he'd gone too far with Keegan. Is that it? Did he do something to him? Something that he had to cover up? Something Aaron might have helped him cover up?

Maybe I should stay away from him. But I know that's not going to happen. No. Tad hasn't discouraged me from seeing him. Just made me more curious than ever.

***

Aaron groans as he pierces into me. My wrists are bound over my head in Velcro cuffs that are affixed to the rod in his wardrobe. He hoists me up the way Brad did in the bathroom a few nights earlier. I close my eyes, doing my best to pretend he's Brad. It helps make the experience more enjoyable, but it's not the same. Aaron's cock is plenty big enough, but the passion just isn't there. And knowing that he's the reason I can't be with Brad just makes it that much more torturous.

He licks across my face like a dog as my ass bounces against his hips.

My wrists strain in the cuffs.

I almost decided not to come over tonight, but he's the only thing keeping me close to Brad—the only chance I have of having him again. So I'll do what I have to.

Sweat rushes down my forehead as he hits my prostate.

I understand why he doesn't want to betray Aaron, but it doesn't change the way I feel about him. Or what I want from him.

Jesse went to stay with his parents' for the weekend, so as far as I know, Brad's free. He typically heads to the showers around nine thirty—something I know from when we were still hooking up. It hasn't been that long since he called it off. A little over a week. But it feels like forever.

I'll have a chance to get what I want. As much as he tries to deny me, he can only repress his feelings for so long. If he feels half as empty as I do without our encounters, it'll be impossible for him to refuse me tonight.

Despite Tad's warning, I can't believe that Brad would do anything to hurt me. But what if he killed Keegan? What if he's more dangerous than I realize?

Then I guess I'm in a shitload of trouble.

"Beg me to come in you," Aaron demands.

"Please...please come in me," I say, but I notice how different it sounds with him than when Brad fucks me.

He cries out, his face mashed in an angry glare as he shoots inside me.

I play as enthralled as I would be if it were Brad, and he lowers me, pulls out, and sucks my dick.

I imagine Brad fucking me from behind. His rough touch across my body. Him throwing me around like I weigh nothing. Spitting in my face.

The pressure in me builds until I come in Aaron's mouth.

He greedily sucks it up and licks my cock.

***

I head into the showers, waiting for Brad to make his entrance. Aaron thinks I'm heading home, but I only get these hookup sessions twice a week, so this is my only chance. Presumably, Aaron's busy fucking a few of my fellow pledges on the other days. It only pisses me off now that my nights with him are the only opportunities I have to get near Brad. If I don't catch him tonight, I'll have to wait at least a few days before I get another opportunity.

I remove my clothes and hide in one of the shower stalls, turning on the water and wetting myself so I'll look like any other brother if one comes in. When I hear someone enter, I peer around the curtain to see if it's him. With a towel over his shoulder, Brad heads to a locker in a nook across from my shower and strips. I should let him know I'm here, but I want to watch him. He pulls off his shirt, revealing the defined lines in his body. I envy those sculpted pecs. His chiseled abs. His height. All the things about him that the gods of genetics have bestowed upon him.

He pulls down his pants, his girth dangling between his thighs. He's a statue of a man—the sort that should be recreated in stone so others have the gift of appreciating his beauty.

Again, I wonder if he might have been involved in Keegan's death.

He retrieves a bag from his locker and takes it into the adjoining stall.

I turn off the water in mine, slip through the side of the curtain, and step into his stall.

"What the fuck?" he asks, turning to me with wide eyes as he looks at me like the stalker I am.

I don't bother with an explanation. Just plant a kiss. One I hope will do the trick. He kisses back and pushes me against the tile wall. Whatever alarm I stirred when he initially saw me has dissipated.

He reveals his feelings through each kiss from my lips down to my chest.

"No, fuck, no," he says between pecks. He offers the occasional lick. Like he just needs to taste my flesh. His lips return to mine. He cups my back with his hand and pulls me flush with him so that I can feel his dick hardening against me. My skin is on fire from the energy he ignites within me.

The sound of the door opening.

"Hey, Brad."

It's Aaron's voice.

Brad hurries to the curtain, opens it, and peers out.

"Hey, man. What's up?"

"Just wanted to catch you before you headed to bed. Are you game to help Alex with the mixer on Friday?"

"Yeah. Totally."

"Perfect."

My attention fixates on Brad's cock. The length. The width. The veins bulging through the swollen flesh.

I want it in my mouth. I want him to come all over my face. And within my ass too. He's the kind of guy I would date just so he could do whatever he wanted with that.

They discuss a few particulars about the next mixer before Aaron leaves. Brad turns back to me, his face white. I can tell by his expression that he doesn't want to follow through with this, so I kneel down and shove his dick in my mouth, hoping he won't be able to resist me. He leans back against the wall. Running his hands through my hair, he grips tightly and forces me to take his cock until I choke on it. I suspect he's punishing me for our transgression against Aaron. I gag, but he holds me in place, forcing me to relax into it.

"Shit, shit," he mutters. I can hear his regret. He wishes he had some self-control. I, on the other hand, don't give a fuck about Aaron. He's been useful, but other than that he's an ass who doesn't have a right to claim me. Right now, he's just an obstacle.

He forces my head back, pulls me to my feet, and pushes me against the opposite wall. He leans down, reaches between my legs, and slides his finger into my hole. His face is stern as he says, "He's been in you already tonight."

I nod. He curses.

"That's the only way I could get in here."

He sucks on my nipple while he shoves two fingers within me.

My dick hardens. It's too hard. He doesn't give me much time to adjust to his digits before he adds a third. I groan.

He looks up to me, fury in his eyes, as though he's pissed that he's getting Aaron's sloppy seconds. He moves in and out of me. I lean back against the tile. I need to just take it. I deserve to be punished for how stupid I've been through all this. How I've made it so hard for us to keep this up.

He pushes in so deep that the pain ripples through my body, making me shiver and tremble. He takes that as an invitation to push in even deeper.

I open my mouth to scream, but I don't want to draw attention in case a brother is nearby.

He leans back and watches me as he continues his work, his face locked in a judgmental glare.

"How is he?" he asks.

"I don't want him. I want you."

"Don't fucking say that," he says, driving his hand farther within me.

"Jesus fucking Christ," I mutter, wishing I could shout it.

He pulls out slightly, granting me some relief, but then pushes back in as quickly as the first time. His expression shifts to something sad. Like he can feel the remnants of Aaron that linger within me. Maybe because he wants me for himself. Maybe because it reminds him that what he's doing against his friend. Maybe because he's thinking about whatever he did with Keegan.

I hear the door outside the bathroom.

He jams within me and covers my mouth with his other hand. It's a good thing he gagged me because the pain was too much for me to quiet myself.

Through a crack in the curtain, I see one of the brothers walk to the counter beside the locker nook. He whistles as Brad digs even deeper. Like he's challenging me. Seeing if I can keep quiet. My ass feels like it's about to split in two.

Brad glares as he continues forcing his entry. Like he's trying to ruin me for anyone else. And it's his hole to ruin.

Despite shifting my ass about to alleviate the pain, my dick is hard.

I hear the brother outside get into the shower beside us— the one I hid in before Brad entered.

Brad pulls his fingers out and flips me around. Pressing me against the wall, he forces himself inside me. I would have thought, between Aaron fucking me and Brad's hand opening me up, I wouldn't have difficulty, but he's too big for it to ever be effortless. My dick swells against the tile. Between the pressure and how hard it is, my cock burns.

Brad moves slowly, but his thrusts are strong. He grabs my wrist and pulls it behind me.

I'm shaking in anticipation from the pain before he twists it sharply. As it smarts, I know I deserve this. For how much I crave him. For how badly I've always really wanted to be hurt like this. For how much all those other guys didn't count because they didn't make me suffer the way he does.

He keeps twisting. I stick my forearm in my mouth and bite down to keep from articulating my pain.

Come on, Brad. You can hurt me worse than that.

Then he does, and I regret my mental request. Is he going to rip my arm off? Although, the way he pushes within me is just as bad. The sting becomes so intense that I slam my head against the tile. It brings me some relief.

The sound of water slapping against the guy in the next stall arouses me even more. It feels as if he's somehow a witness to our passion.

Brad lets go of my arm and pulls out of me.

I turn back to him, and he pushes me back against the wall once again, gripping onto my cock and stroking violently.

His hands are so dry that he's tearing at my tender flesh, but I don't care.

And then that familiar sensation. Like a surge of electricity shooting through my pelvis. I grab his wrist to stop him. I want him to come first, but he clings on, refusing to stop. I look to him, mentally pleading for him to release me, but he continues and my come pours across the back of his hand.

I come. And come. The energy that rushes through me is so powerful that I throw myself back against the tile a few times before settling. What come doesn't end up on the back of Brad's hand, he collects in his palm before lifting his hand to my face and pushing his fingers into my mouth. I lick it up. I'm about to swallow when he grabs my jaw firmly and shakes his head.

He kisses me and sucks my seed back up. Once he gathers it all, he leans back and swishes it around in his mouth. He spits it in his palm and massages it across his cock.

"Put your arms around me," he whispers.

He steps forward. Jumping, I wrap my legs around his waist and my arms around his neck. He grips onto my thigh and navigates into me, his entry much smoother this time because of how much my hole has been through these past few minutes. Holding me in place, he squats and bounces me in his lap. He cringes, biting down. I wonder if it's to keep from screaming. He grunts softly as I can tell he's coming.

As he continues his sharp movements, he kisses me, throwing us off balance so that he falls forward. He catches himself, but not before knocking the back of my head against the tile.

I shout out. He clasps his hand over my mouth, but it's too late.

The water in the adjoining stall turns off.

"You okay, dude?" the guy asks.

"Yeah. Just me, Brad. Just slipped on the soap."

The brother laughs. "Damn, dude. That would've been a real bitch if you'd have fallen."

"Right?"

The pitter patter of feet.

Brad pulls out of me and sets me down. He urges me into a corner close to the curtain and opens the other side.

"How've you been, Howard?" he asks.

"Pretty good," Howard replies as he moseys to the lockers.

They chat up some shit about their last football game, so I assume they're on the team together.

The brother collects his belongings, and when he finally leaves, Brad attacks me with a kiss.

BRAD

I wouldn't do this to my buddy. Not intentionally.

We lie in my bed together, Ian resting on my chest as I cling to him. After a few fucking and jerk-off sessions we've shared since he snuck up on me in the showers, he fell asleep. Pissed as I am that he surprised me, I'm relieved that he's quieted the agonizing pain I've felt since I tried to push him away. I'm tired of trying to convince myself I don't want him.

But what about Aaron? How am I supposed to tell him I'm the asshole making moves on his trick? I need to come clean.

I gaze down at Ian. The pink marks I made around his neck will likely turn black and blue within the next few days. As soon as I got him in here, I couldn't control myself. I stroke my hand up and down his tight, compact abs. His body is so little. Appears so fragile. More fragile than it really is.

It reminds me of how fragile Keegan was. He wanted it just as badly. Begged for it. I gave it to him the best way I could. Even when I knew it was wrong. Even when I lost control. That was the night I discovered there was something truly wicked within me. Something far more dangerous than I ever imagined. That's who I want to protect Ian from. I can't ever let it get that bad again. But the feelings I have for him are even stronger than the ones I had for Keegan.

As I gaze at his beautiful face, all I can think about is how I want him to be mine.

He stirs, his arms tightening around me as if he's holding on to me to make sure he's safe. Safety isn't something I can offer, though. But how many times do I have to tell him that? Why is he so self-destructive? Is it really because of the accident with his brother? The investigator I hired told me it was a gun in his aunt's and uncle's closet. When he went into their bedroom, his six-year-old brother was there. Didn't know the difference between it and a toy gun. Ian tried to take it from him, but the kid thought they were playing, and in their fight over it, the gun went off. His brother died in his arms. Enough to fuck anyone up, but how could Ian blame himself for something that clearly wasn't his fault? How could he believe he deserved to hurt over something like that? He doesn't. He's not a monster. Not like I am.

His eyelids flutter as he wakes. I don't pretend I'm not staring at him. I wait for him to be freaked out by it, but he just asks, "Do you want me to go?"

"No," I say quickly.

"What's wrong?"

"I just feel like this—whatever it is—is happening too fast."

"I think I know what this is really about."

But he can't know.

"Keegan."

"What?"

"It's okay. Tad was drunk, and he mentioned that you guys hooked up."

Blood rushes to my face. Tad didn't have any right to tell him that.

"I'm sorry," he says. "I'm just trying to make sense of why the hell you're so weird about us."

Silence. He knows more than he's saying. I just wish he'd fucking say what's on his mind.

"Brad, the reason that you're like this with us. It doesn't have anything to do with Keegan, does it? Anything to do with something that might have happened?"

"God-fucking-dammit!" I bash my fist against the mattress. He rises and scoots away from me quickly. It's the first time that I've seen him afraid. Truly afraid of me, and I feel like shit about it.

"No, wait," I say quickly. He sits erect. Not moving. Like he's worried if he does something that I'll lose it.

"Ian, I didn't mean to hurt him."

The expression on his face suggests he wasn't expecting me to admit it. But he's cornered me. Now he knows about Keegan. About what we were doing. And about my suspicious behavior with him.

I'm shit out of luck.

I should keep my dumb mouth shut, but since he's bound to get there on his own, I want to tell him the truth. Maybe if I tell him, he'll finally get a clue and leave me the fuck alone. Maybe he'll tell the police, and I'll get what I deserve. Maybe that's what needs to happen. Maybe it hasn't been worth it keeping this secret.

"He was a pledge," I say. "Just like you. We were hooking up pretty regularly, and he needed it all the fucking time. He liked everything. Punching. Slapping. But his favorite was asphyxiation. And I liked it that way too. He had this collar that he'd want me to put around his neck. We had a safety signal to make sure we never took things too far. The night of his...*suicide*...things got out of hand."

"Oh my God."

"That day, I found out Keegan had been hooking up with one of the other brothers. Roger Madders. Doing it the whole time we were together. Didn't tell either of us. We both evidently are a little rougher in the sack. I was going to call Keegan out that night, after we... Because I wanted to make him pay for what he'd done. I wanted to really unleash it on him. I admit, I had too much to fucking drink that night, and I blacked out. I don't really know what happened after we started getting into it. I just woke up, and he was lying there. Not moving. Not breathing."

"Then it was an accident."

"I'm not sure. Sometimes when I get mad, or even just when I'm having sex, there's this fucking anger that builds up in me. And I don't know that I can control it. Maybe I really wanted to kill him. Maybe I did right before I fucking blacked out."

"And you covered it up?"

"Aaron found us. When I told him what happened, he helped me cover it up. That's why I owe him. That's why I've been fighting this so hard."

He doesn't look as concerned as he should, and it makes me believe he's as fucking suicidal as the day we met at orientation.

"Ian, please. If you know what's good for you..."

"You made a fucking mistake. A really *really* shitty one for not going to the police...and covering it up to look like a suicide like a fucking psychopath. But I don't think you meant to kill him."

"How can you know that?"

"If you had, why would you be telling me this?"

He offers a kiss. Like he's trying to tell me that he believes me. That he trusts me. I accept it because it soothes me from the pain of everything I've been carrying with me. My horrible mistakes. My sins.

Tears rush from the corners of my eyes.

I'm ashamed. I pull away and turn from him, but he snatches my face and forces me to look at him.

"Let go of me," I say as I snatch his wrist with a force that must remind him of the darkness within me.

"I've done too much to get this far with you for you to fucking give me this bullshit," he says. "If you don't want to fuck me, that's one thing. But if it's this crap you're carrying around from the past, then you need to get over it. Because I'm not going to make your life easy as long as I have a chance. I'm going to keep coming here and harassing you. I'm going to find out when you're alone. And you won't be able to stop this anymore than you have already."

"Fuck you," I say before I kiss him again.

I thought after I told him the truth he would be freaked out. That he'd leave. But having him here, knowing the truth, fills me with a relief and passion unlike anything I've experienced with him before. I can't pretend not to like him right now.

I pull away and offer bites down his body. Licking occasionally.

His flesh. His sweat. It all tastes so good.

He writhes in pleasure, his dick growing once again.

I take it into my mouth and suck and lick and tease. It's one of the few times I've given him something other than pain. It feels good to give him pleasure, but just as soon as I feel his dick grow even more, I'm compelled by the instincts within me to release it. Pushing him onto his side, I get on my knees and force myself within him. I punch his ass. It isn't a soft punch. I can see in his eyes that it's just what he wants.

"You stupid motherfucker," I say before spitting on his cheek.

He tosses his head back as I raid his body, filled with a new sort of passion. And a sense of freedom from having revealed my nightmare to him.

AARON

Fucking traitor.

My belt is tied around my neck, the end trapped in my closet door as I choke on it. Heat swells in my face as I perform an angry self-service.

I stew over the twisted betrayal of someone I thought was my friend.

Ian seemed preoccupied tonight. Since Brad hadn't come up with any leads, I figured I'd follow him to find out what he was up to. Little did I know I didn't need to go very far to discover the truth. Ian led me to the showers, where I stood on the step in the handicapped stall and waited for whoever it was to enter. It was a brother, and whoever it was would pay for their deception. When I saw Brad enter, I was disturbed. Beyond disturbed. Horrified.

Again?

Was Ian another Keegan?

Keegan had played us both like a real champ, and now here this new kid was doing it all over again. Only this time, it was worse because Brad knew what was up. With Keegan, I knew about Brad, but I worked to take him away. To make him mine. I liked him. And why the fuck did Brad deserve a hot piece of ass like that?

Neither of us had won that game, though.

This seemed a strange sort of revenge that Brad was playing on me, making me wonder if maybe he knew about what Keegan and I did behind his back. Although, if Brad knew the truth, he wouldn't have just taken Ian from me. He would've killed me.

To be betrayed by, not only a brother, but a friend who I helped out of jam—who I bailed out of what he believed could have been his worst nightmare—hurts like a fucking bitch.

I recall another betrayal. Archon Jeffery. My freshman year as a pledge, I fell for the gym rat quarterback who constantly strutted around the house without a shirt on like he was shoving his beautiful form in all our faces. He was particularly attentive to me, and I loved the attention. I wanted him so bad. But he had a girlfriend, so I never pushed. One night, he led me to believe he was driving me to a ritual. Instead, he pulled over, and while I was bound, took me in the most brutal and unforgiving of ways. The pain, the cruelty cut me so deep. But I believed that meant he wanted me, and despite what he'd done, I still wanted him. To my surprise, when I attempted to pursue him, he rejected me. Made me feel like an idiot for thinking he could feel that way about another guy. I felt defiled. Violated. And I fucking hated him.

Betrayal always stings. It tears into the heart.

I rub my cock so hard it feels like it's on fire. I didn't lube up. I should have, but it's too late for regret. I rub and rub until my dick's raw. I bite down on my lip as the pressure in my face continues to build, the belt pinching against my skin. Spots appear before me as I imagine making Brad and

Ian pay for their deceit. I imagine contriving a way to get them back for how they've duped me. That's what they fucking deserve.

I groan as much as my constricted throat allows. My load spews out before me onto the carpet.

6

JESSE

I head into the warehouse. This is where my big brother Alex said we needed to meet. It's the same warehouse the brothers brought me for one of the nights when the guys made us strip to our underwear and wrestle in a kiddie pool filled with mud. Would've been a good night to wear boxers instead of briefs. Considering the sorts of rituals we've endured, I'm spooked about having to come out here. I fear there'll be some serious hazing going down tonight. Will I end up on the news as a pledge who ended up the victim of a violent hazing?

"Hey, Jesse," a voice comes from a dark corner. I recognize it, but it isn't Alex.

Aaron steps out of a shadow into an orange shaft of light that pours through a window on the side of the warehouse. He has a pleased look on his face. He wears black slacks and a white button-up with the sleeves rolled up. With the end of the wave in his bangs twisted into its signature curl, he looks like he's about to head to a party.

"What do I need to do?" I ask.

"This isn't about being a pledge, Jesse. This is a house call. More someone trying to make sure you get what you need."

"What do you mean?"

"Ian's your friend, right?"

"Best friend."

"You don't think he would ever lie to you...or steal from you, do you?"

"Never."

Why would he even ask me that?

"How much do you like Brad?"

"What does he have to do with anything?"

He sticks his hands in his pockets and walks around me. He moves slowly as he looks off like he's thinking hard about something.

"Just answer the question. I've seen you guys together. You make a cute couple."

I beam. I can't help it. I've had a crush on him since we started seeing each other. I know it's still just fucking for now, but I've pushed. I want him to make a move. To tell me that he wants there to be something more between us.

"Yeah."

"Has he not asked you to do anything more serious?"

"No."

He stops his walk around me.

"Oh, then maybe I'm just confused," he says.

"About what?"

I don't like his evasiveness. He didn't get me to come all the way out here for nothing.

"So, you don't know that Ian and Brad have been..."

My cheeks fill with heat.

"No they haven't," I insist.

It's something Aaron's using to get me to react angrily toward my friend. It's a vicious prank. But I can't help but fear it might be true. If it is, I'll fucking scratch Ian's eyes out. Not once in all the times I've talked to him about Brad has he expressed an interest in him. He's acted like Brad's the last guy in the world he'd ever consider fucking. Has that been part of the deception, though? Has he been trying to conceal his interest by seeming impossibly uninterested? That would make more sense. Brad's breathtakingly hot. The kind of hot a guy would want to fuck even if he was a total asshole.

Once again, I'm reminded that Ian's always the one they like. I remember Jared in high school. How he pursued me. How he pushed. And then how he ended up writing love letters to Ian. Ian revealed his trustworthiness by showing me the letters, but I couldn't help but resent him. Hate him for knowing that he had stolen the heart of the guy I wanted. Jared was just the first in a stream of guys I would catch gazing fondly at Ian whenever we all hung out together. They glowed when he entered a room. I wished they would have glowed for me when I entered a room. And I don't believe it's ever just been about his looks. There's something about him. Something guys are naturally drawn to. I've never been able to place it. But it's always been there. Taunting me. Mocking me.

Despite these insecurities, I can't understand why he would want to fuck Brad when he has Aaron.

I curb my suspicion, hoping Ian's hiding somewhere nearby and that Aaron will reveal this for the game it really is.

Aaron smirks in a way that concerns me even more.

"Jesse, really? You're not a dumb kid. I don't blame you for trusting him because Ian had me fooled too. I think he was just using me to get into Alpha Theta Mu, you know? Now that he's in, he's going to move on to Brad. I didn't know if maybe you guys had a past where maybe he was jealous of you..."

Was that it? Now that I finally had someone for myself—someone who hadn't shown any interest in him—he was trying to take him from me?

"When I see him—" I begin.

"Wait a second, Jesse. I know what you're thinking. You want to run to him and get into a fight. Make a scene. Let me play this out for you. You run to Ian. Yell at him about how you feel about what he's done. How mad you are that he's been doing all this behind your back. What happens? He defends himself. He apologizes. You never talk again. He runs to Brad. Doesn't really need a friend now that he's with one of the hottest guys on campus."

Ian wouldn't betray me in such an inconsiderate way. But if he really is fucking Brad behind my back, then I must be wrong.

"If you want this to play out in your favor, you have to play smart. We can both be winners in this."

"How?"

I'm still not convinced Ian's deceived me, but if I find out it's true, I'm getting him.

"He's lying to you. Doing all this behind your back. Cheating you out of something that you want. So what if you cheat him out of what he wants? What if you push things the other way a little?"

"What do you mean?"

I can tell that he's thinking of something devious. Something that might extend beyond anything I'd be willing to do to Ian even if he's been a total motherfucker.

"What if we got Ian a little drunk? Made him look like he was hooking up with someone? And maybe Brad just happened to walk in on him? We could do it at the mixer this Friday."

"Who's going to do this?"

"I got a friend I can bribe."

"Why do you want to do this?"

"I want Ian. And Brad did me wrong, too. He acted like he was there for me. And when I suspected that Ian was running a game on me, I got him to check in to see what was up. Only problem was, Brad was the one he was running around with. Call me stupid, though, for trusting Brad because he's done this before. Fool me twice, shame on me, right? Jesse, we've both been fools. Ian fucked you over, and if you can just push things a little, Brad will go back to you."

"I don't know."

"What's the issue?"

"It's shitty and all. Like I may never talk to that fucker again after this. But if they really like each other, I don't want to get in the way of that."

"They don't!" Aaron says in such a severe tone that it makes me stand erect, worried that he's about to jump me. He's always so cool and collected. I haven't seen him lose his shit before.

He takes a breath. "Brad likes him because the other guys do. That's it. He's just a plaything that he'll enjoy for a little while. As long as everyone's infatuated. The moment he's a regular brother like everyone else, his interest will wane. I've seen it happen again and again."

Do the guys not like me?

"Jesse," he says, approaching me and setting his hand on my shoulder. "You're an amazing guy. I think you'd be good for Brad. You're honest. Loyal. You're not the one running around trying to deceive anyone. What he's doing is shitty, but like you said, you haven't exactly established that you're boyfriends or anything. Brad sees it as having two options right now, and the moment he senses that one of those is off the table, he'll turn to you."

"What if he doesn't want to be with me?"

"Then at least you have a fair shot at making it work. Isn't that what everyone deserves?"

I do deserve that.

"And Ian won't find out that I'm involved?" I ask.

His lips curl up at the edges as if he's about to smile. He must be feeling the same sort of satisfaction I'm feeling about evening the score.

But I'm sad. Not just because of Brad, but because I've lost a friend. My best friend. He betrayed me. Whatever comes next, he deserves because he did all this at the expense of our friendship.

7

IAN

Brad's telling Aaron about us tonight, and I'm telling Jesse. We can't keep this secret from them anymore. What we've been doing behind their backs has been wrong. When the truth comes out, Jesse will be pissed. I only hope we can find a way to repair our friendship.

Jesse is wide-eyed as we drink Jell-O shots together on the back porch of the Alpha Theta Mu house. On the other side of the party, Brad sets up a makeshift bar on a card table with some of the brothers. We've agreed to meet up after we've talked to our respective friends.

I'm definitely waiting until I get a few drinks in Jesse before I say anything.

"Hey, Jesse," Alex says as he steps out the back door, carrying a keg. "Give us a hand?"

As Jesse hurries to his big brother's aid, through the crowd of brothers and Gamma Theta sisters, I spy Roger a few yards away, slouched in a couch that I helped some of the other pledges set up in the yard earlier today. In a navy polo and a backwards Alpha Theta Mu cap, he takes a hit from a bong. I've only seen him a few times at meetings and parties. He doesn't live at the main Alpha Theta Mu house, so he's less visible than some of the other brothers. Considering every fraternity event he's missed, I imagine he's accrued a substantial amount in fines, but I doubt the fraternity will complain when his hedge fund manager father is eager to pay them off on his son's behalf.

Since I heard Brad's version of the night Keegan died, I've been curious to talk to him. If they were hooking up, then he must be suspicious about what happened that night.

I feel bad for the guy. One day he was fucking Keegan, who he could have liked as more than a trick. And the next day, Keegan was dead.

I sit beside him on the couch. He turns to me, his red irises sparkling. I consider bailing, but I'm too curious to walk away.

"Newbie?" he asks, scanning me over with obvious interest.

"Yeah."

He offers me a hit, which I accept. Then he reclines back, spreading his legs, his dick hard as a rock in his cargo shorts.

He squints. "Aren't you Aaron's boy?" he asks.

"I've been hooking up with him, if that's what you mean."

He pulls his legs back together. "Then fuck off."

"You always so uninterested in guys who are hooking up with your brothers?"

"I don't do the incest thing."

"That's not what I've heard."

His face flushes. He glances either way, as though he's determining whether or not anyone else heard me. He stands and starts off, muttering, "Follow me, kid."

I'm worried about following some stoner, but considering his reaction to my statement, I'm too curious not to. He leads me to a bathroom in the house. Once I'm inside, he shuts the door behind me, grips my throat, and shoves me back against the wall.

"Is Aaron talking shit about what happened between me and Keegan?" he asks. He squeezes my throat, constricting my breath.

I can't tell if the red in his eyes is from the high or his rage.

"Aaron?" I ask as he loosens his grip.

What the fuck does Aaron have to do with this? Does Roger know that Aaron helped Brad cover up Keegan's death?

"Should have fucking known he'd blab to whatever newbie. You don't say shit to anyone about what happened between us. You got that?"

"Wait. He just told me that you and Brad were fucking around with Keegan."

I hope my lie will elicit some more intel.

"Oh really? Trying to make it all about us? He got his piece of ass too, so if he's trying to pin shit on anyone, he was doing just as much as the rest of us. What has he told you about that night?"

"Nothing."

He squeezes my throat again. If Keegan liked to be choked, Roger was the guy to choke him.

"Bullshit. He obviously told you something."

A knock at the door.

"Blow me!" Roger shouts, then returns his attention to me, his eyes filled with suspicion: "Did Aaron show you the letter?"

I shake my head. He releases my throat and rubs his hands across his face. "Shit. I shouldn't even be talking to you about this. Just pretend I haven't said anything. I don't want any part of this. That kid did all this to himself."

"Did he deserve to die because of what he did?" I ask.

His eyes water, but I can't tell if it's from how high he is or from talking about Keegan.

"No, he didn't. I loved that fucking asshole!" Now I know why he's crying. "But after Aaron told me that shit about what he was doing behind my back—with Brad, with him—I just couldn't. What he did cut me like a knife. I told him to fuck off, but I was going to take him back. He must have known that. We weren't exclusive. He hadn't done anything wrong, but then the dumbass went and—"

Another knock.

He turns to the door and slams his fist against it repeatedly, the curly locks draping down his forehead shaking with each blow. "Do you have a death wish?"

The guy on the other side of the door curses.

Roger whispers to himself, "How the fuck did I know what Keegan was going to do? That he was going to lose his shit like that?"

I still can't make sense of what he's talking about, but I'm afraid to press because I feel one misstep and he'll catch on to how little I really know, which is just that Aaron seems suspiciously involved in Brad's and Roger's accounts of that night. Makes me wonder if he played a greater role in this than either are aware.

"You didn't mention anything to the police about this?" I ask.

"What? Oh, yeah, so it could get back to my parents that I'm a faggot? My uncle works at the Atlanta Police Department, and he's one of the biggest homophobes in the world. Hell, Aaron hiding Keegan's letter saved my fucking reputation. Not all of us can be Aaron Morgans or Brad Raegers. Some of us have families that are still trapped in the dark ages with books that say we should be stoned."

"Hey!" a slurred voice calls from the other side of the door. "When the fuck are you going to be done in there?"

The guy's words pull Roger's attention from me. He glances around uneasily, as if he realizes he's said too much. He darts out of the bathroom, leaving me reeling in a sea of questions.

Not much of what he said makes sense, but I have an idea of where I can find some answers.

***

I raid Aaron's room. I'm familiar with all the little hiding places he uses for his toys and lube. He's been running around all night for the mixer, so he's too busy to come in here. Since Roger was worried that Aaron had shown me a letter, I know what I'm looking for. After some searching, I notice Aaron's fraternity bible on his desk. I have my own copy from Tad. It contains the history and bylaws of the fraternity. All the pledges have to borrow one, study up on it, and endure pop quizzes until initiation. It would be the perfect hiding place for a letter. I riffle through it until I notice a sheet of loose-leaf notebook paper.

Roger,

When I approached you today, I wasn't expecting rejection. Since we met during rush, and I approached you and asked if you could help me find a can to throw up in, I knew by the look in your eyes that there was something there. A connection. Something that I can't believe was just us. It was like some otherworldly force had brought us together. Orchestrated every life circumstance that I'd ever experienced so that I could have that moment with you. I can't say I'm innocent of shit, but neither can you. And I've never felt for anyone else the way I've felt for you, you stupid shit.

Every day that we talked, every day that we did anything, meant so much to me. I loved waiting for you to curl up with me when you were high because you're always more affectionate like that. And I always wanted you to hold me a little closer. Kiss me a little softer. Don't get me wrong. I like the other stuff just fine, but those tender moments always made me know in the rougher ones that you really did care about me.

At least, that's what I thought. I can't live knowing that you hate me. Knowing that you don't want to be with me. I don't know what's fucked up in my head that I misread us. That I thought you cared for me the way I care for you, but I can't bear it. I can't deal with the pain anymore. It's always hurt. The world's always felt like shit, but I thought at least with you that burning pain in my chest wouldn't feel so bad. But if I can't have this, then I don't have anything. When Aaron gives you this note, I'll be gone, but I hope that, even if you didn't love me, you at least know that I love you. Everything about you. Totally and completely, and each night we shared, I imagined a future with you. I'm just sorry that I was so disappointing that you couldn't do the same to me.

Yours forever,

Keegan

My eyes water a little. It's tragic thinking this guy cared so much about Roger, who so clearly cared about him too.

What really happened that night? Did Keegan refuse to use the safety signal so that Brad would accidentally kill him? And why didn't Aaron tell Brad about the letter? Was he protecting Roger from being outed by it? Or were their darker motives behind his involvement? He was fucking Keegan too, after all. Something Brad didn't know. Or at least, didn't tell me he knew.

Whatever the reason, I need to get this letter to Brad. And he, Roger, and Aaron need to have it out until they figure out what really went down that night.

JESSE

I head down the hall to Aaron's room. It's the last place I can think to look for Ian. I was supposed to keep tabs on him, and had Alex not asked me to help him and some of the other brothers with the kegs they brought, I would have done a good job.

Aaron gave me this drink to give him. Said he roofied it. When Ian passes out, we'll take him somewhere and make it look like he's fucking another guy—one that Aaron will be bribing shortly.

I carry two shot glasses. One for me, and one for Ian.

Since I talked to Aaron, Brad's avoided meeting up with me, and now I know it's because he's got the hots for Ian.

I don't want to do this to my friend, but I feel that I have to just to get him back for how wrong he's done me.

The door to Aaron's room opens and Ian steps out, a concerned look on his face. He tucks a sheet of paper into his back pocket and turns to me.

"Where the fuck have you been?" I ask.

"Hey, man. I just have something I have to take care of real quick."

As he tries to pass me, I step in front of him.

"Ian, what's wrong?"

"Nothing."

I want him to be honest. To tell me what's been going on. If he does, I'll toss this shot and tell Aaron I can't go through with it.

"Ian, there's been something going on for a while. You don't act like yourself anymore. We've hardly talked since we pledged. Why don't you talk to me?"

"There is something I have to talk to you about, but can I just have a minute?"

"Why are you being like this?"

"I just need to—"

He tries to pass me, but I block him again.

"Ian—"

"Jesse, I don't have time for this. I'm sorry, but I just don't. I need to find Brad."

Aaron was right. Why does he need a friend when he's with the hottest guy in Alpha Theta Mu? My fury consumes me.

"I just wanted to do a shot with you," I say. "One shot and then you can go do whatever..."

...or whoever.

He sighs and takes the shot from me. He's about to drink it when I clink my plastic shot glass against his.

"To us," I say before we down them together.

He's not the Ian I was friends with when we first came here. He's changed. He deserves our little prank. I doubt it'll be as effective as Aaron suggests, but even if it just makes Brad and Ian pissed at each other for the night, that's good enough for me.

Ian starts down the stairs, and I meander after him because Aaron assured me he won't make it very far.

8

AARON

"He needs it," I say as I pull Roger into an empty dorm room. "Has this whole torture slave-fantasy that he wants to play out."

Roger's eyes sparkle in the lamplight that illuminates the room. He wants this. Bad.

He's been rolling since Keegan's death, making it even easier to play him than it was back then.

Once Brad sees him fucking Ian, it's over. That'll take him right back to the night he found out about what Keegan was doing behind his back.

Keegan's death was amusingly simple. Initially, through checking his phone, I learned that he and Brad were hooking up. I planned on winning him over, but one night while I was going through his computer, I discovered he'd been arranging meetups with Roger on Facebook. From their exchanges, I could tell it was serious. Far more serious than what he was doing with Brad or me. To say I was jealous would be an understatement. My initial determination to win him came from discovering that he was hooking up with Brad behind my back, but when I realized I didn't stand a chance against Roger, something dark within me sprung to life. Like when I watched Archon Jeffery tragically reach his end after I helped him take just a little more of his heroin stash than he was used to. Well, maybe not a little.

I confronted Keegan about his other interests, and as I expected, he made it clear that Roger was the guy he wanted to be with. Unlike Brad, I've always been good at calming the raging spirit within, and so rather than give Keegan what he

153

expected, I acted sympathetic. Like a mentor. Someone he could confide in about his dilemma.

I worked on Roger first, telling him what I had discovered about Keegan. That he was fucking me and Brad behind his back. He was eager for a fight with Keegan, but I encouraged him to an even better way to get revenge. To just call it off without explanation. Tell him he didn't want to see him anymore. After all, what right did Keegan have to an explanation when he had hardly been honest about his extracurricular hookups? So Roger called it off, never telling Keegan about what I'd told him. And when Keegan was at his weakest—broken-hearted and defeated—the door was open for me to soothe his wounds.

The next night, I went to Brad to tell him about what was happening behind his back. We drank and drank, and I drugged him with enough Xanax that I knew he would last just long enough to make a violent attempt with Ian, who I encouraged to ease his pain through another fuck with him. I listened at the door as they did their thing, listening to Brad getting his revenge on Keegan until Brad passed out. When Keegan came to me after, I caressed and loved him before binding and hanging him in my room. Then I pulled him down and dragged him back into Brad's room so that when Brad woke, he discovered me, standing horrified over Keegan's lifeless body, their choker around Keegan's neck. Brad was mortified. And I agreed to be the good friend that I am and hide his wicked deed.

It was a game of dominos, and each one fell perfectly into the next until the very end when I created a believable hanging—the one that Keegan's roommate discovered after the spring formal.

Brad would tell no one because of his involvement in the death, and Roger was easy enough to discourage once he learned of the suicide note I wrote—one that I claimed Keegan had left me to give him. I'd sprinkled some of the details of their relationship—things Keegan had shared when he opened up to me. These details would be enough to convince Roger of the validity of the letter. And of course, being a good friend, I wouldn't let something like that get out to the world. His family, after all, would be horrified when they discovered he's a faggot.

With Brad and Roger unwilling to share the truth, that left Keegan. And he'd never tell...

I was victorious. Against my friends who had captured Keegan's interest, and against that little fuck who thought he could find better than me.

"He's out in the shed in the woods," I say to Roger. "The one where we take the newbies to give them a good time. Made me tie him up there for whoever I could grab to do the job. But I don't trust anyone else to do it."

"This is one of your boys?" he asks, obviously turned off knowing he's getting sloppy seconds.

As I carried Ian to the shed, I noticed him stirring before he vomited down my back, surely tossing up some of the roofie Jesse had doped him up with. But it did what it needed to so I could get him to his torture chamber. Even better, his release assured me he might be somewhat coherent when Roger came for his surprise visit.

"We hooked up once," I say. "I got this other guy I'm working on, so I figured you might have more fun with this one, you know?"

"You got any condoms?"

"Condoms? You think a kid like that wants a condom on?"

I can tell by the face he makes I need to soothe his concern.

"The guy's practically a virgin. Only reason he wants something this fucked up is because he's never tried it."

"And he wants it rough?"

"Don't be easy on him, or he'll just hate you for it. Now, go on. Get to it. And have fun."

I wink, and he smiles and heads off to join Ian at his fate.

I pat a hard bulge in my pocket. After Roger's finished with him, I have a special surprise for my little Ian: a syringe filled with suxamethonium chloride. A Google search told me all I needed to know about the shit. Untraceable. Would take care of the treacherous asshole in under a minute. It was just the trick, and when I told Finn I could sell some and give him a cut of the profits, he was eager to swipe a few bottles from Emory Hospital. Anything for a buck.

There's enough in this syringe to kill three guys.

After Brad and I catch Ian in his deceit against me, Brad will console me back at the house. Then I'll head back out to the shed and stick Ian with this syringe. When he dies, I'll hurry back to Brad and tell him I went back to confront them, but discovered Ian's corpse. Brad will tear Roger apart with his bare hands. And if he doesn't succeed in finishing the job, I have plenty of this suxamethonium chloride to make him believe he did. Then we'll hide the bodies, and Brad will have three deaths on his conscience. Three bodies that will haunt him for the rest of his life.

This is the final act, not just the end of Ian, but the torture of the guy I'm really out to get—the supposed friend who betrayed me twice. Who won twice.

But he won't be winning after tonight.

IAN

I wake from my blackout.

Fuck.

How many drinks did I have? That shot Jesse gave me must have put me over the edge.

I recall my mission and stir to life, but my arms are over my head, my wrists locked in place. I struggle with them, but as my vision clears, I see they're bound to a rod in a corner.

Where the fuck am I?

My head aches. A rancid taste fills my mouth. Like I just blew chunks.

I search around.

Decrepit shelves line an adjacent wall. Hay and wood chips are scattered across the concrete floor. In a window a few feet from me, I catch the reflection of an open door leading out to the woods. I'm in some sort of shed. A draft catches my attention, and I notice that I'm not wearing any pants. Concern rises within me, but I'm too disoriented to do much more than continue struggling with my wrists. Searching desperately for a way out, a powerful sensation sweeps through me before I vomit, the residue filling a gag in my mouth. Since it doesn't have a way of seeping through the gag, I choke on it. I spit until it spills through cracks in the edges of the gag. As I try to remember how I ended up in this place, I recall moments of consciousness that seem like a dream.

I bounced up and down, looking around to see what was happening when I saw Aaron was carrying me over his shoulder. I assumed I blacked out outside and he was taking me back to the house. The bouncing was so intense that I became nauseated and vomited before blacking out again.

The memory assures me of who the real villain is here. Did he find out about Brad and me? Is this some sort of punishment?

My vision blurred, my senses numbed from what feels like a night of far too much drinking, I struggle to get free.

What feels like minutes pass before I hear a sound behind me. I turn and see Roger standing in the doorway, his face illuminated with moonlight. As he enters, I can tell by his slow movements that he's out of it. Wasted. Stoned. He has a wicked expression on his face. The sort I imagine he used to give Keegan before he would fuck the shit out of him.

I squirm about, crying for help, but my intent must not be clear because he approaches and strokes his hand up and down my leg in a way that I know exactly where this is heading, and I suspect Aaron played a large part in how I ended up here.

My cheeks flush as my thoughts align with a horrifying realization. Aaron and Roger are working together. They did something to Keegan and convinced Brad that it was his fault. Now I'm their next victim.

Roger pets my leg, and I shift about, but he wraps his arm around me to hold me in place as he strokes his cock.

"Oh, you like it real dirty, don't you, you nasty bitch?"

It reminds me of when I tried to get Aaron's attention that first night when he bound me. I'm struggling, but I think that's just turning him on even more. He wets his dick with some saliva and then forces into me.

As I cry out, I vomit again and work to spit it out through what little spaces are between the gag and my mouth.

The sensation in my ass intensifies. He's big. A lot bigger than Brad.

As I realize he's not giving in and my efforts are just making it harder on myself, I settle into the pain, assisting him because I know that's the only way I'm going to make it through this without my insides being ripped apart.

BRAD

"I know what he's up to," Aaron says. "Saw him heading out here. Acting all shady. It's that fucking guy. He's going to meet him out here."

"I don't think so," I say. "That's what I've been wanting to talk to you about."

"Just be quiet for a minute, okay? If he fucking hears us, he's going to run off, and I don't want him to get the satisfaction of thinking he's getting away with something."

He ducks as he guides me through the foliage, dodging low-hanging branches as we creep alongside the old shed. It's a place I'm familiar with from hooking up here with some of my own tricks.

I hear what sounds like someone panting in the shed. Someone's hooking up in there, but Aaron's made a mistake if he thinks it's Ian. We've agreed to be exclusive. Haven't even hooked up with Jesse or Aaron since our last conversation.

Aaron walks past the edge of the woods and approaches the shed, looking into the open doorway.

He's still. Silent. He doesn't look like he's seen something that contradicts what he thought was happening, but like he's caught Ian in the act.

I creep from the woods and check inside the shed.

"Motherfucker," Aaron mutters as he steps aside. It's clear he just can't look at it anymore, but I'm stunned.

Roger's fucking someone, but the shadow in the corner is so dark that I can't be sure it's Ian.

I try to convince myself that it can't be.

IAN

The pain within me hurts so much. I keep reminding myself to relax. Any resistance I offer is only going to make it worse. I know I can take the pain. I've taken worse than this before. My chest burns with a painful ache—from the emotional, not the physical pain—as this guy invades my body.

Tears stream down my cheeks.

It can only last so much longer.

Aaron must've found out about Brad and me, but this seems like too severe a punishment for what we did. And far outside the realm of hazing. It's the sort of thing I'd expect to see on the news about a fraternity prank gone awry.

I peer into the window and see Brad's reflection as he stands in the doorway.

I'm relieved, but the pained expression on his face makes me realize that he's not interpreting the situation correctly. He thinks I want this. Is it because I'm not resisting? I start to squirm, feeling the sting in my hole as my muscles lock, and I fight for my freedom. If I can just make enough movements, he'll see that I need him.

Help me, Brad!

He doesn't move from the doorway.

I chew at my gag like a dog chewing at a bone as I desperately try to loosen it enough that I can cry out. That I can get his attention. If I can just get him to hear me...

BRAD

Roger's backwards cap bounces with his body. With his shorts at his ankles, he shoves into a guy in the corner.

It reminds me of when Aaron told me Keegan and Roger were fucking. Roger can give Ian what he wants. What he needs.

"It's not him," I mutter. But though his face is cast in a shadow, I know from his legs and the polo he's wearing that it's him. His hands bound over his head, he tosses his head back and forth, clearly delighting in having Roger inside him. He's gagged, and I wish I could believe he didn't want it—that Roger was taking him by force—but it's not like Roger would have fucking dragged him back here and tied him up. There are enough fucked up guys like Ian that he wouldn't need to resort to that.

Heat surges to my face. I want to run in there and beat the crap out of Ian, but as Aaron moves closer to me, his face locked in a cringe, I realize there's nothing I can do. Unleashing my rage will only let Aaron know the truth about what we've done. And at this point, why lose a friend over an asshole like Ian?

I swallow my pride.

Fuck you, Ian.

This is my curse. I find fucked up guys who evidently like what Roger and me have to offer.

Why did Ian bother leading me to believe he wanted more when he could have just as easily chosen Roger? Or did he want to fuck both of us? That's what that greedy son of a bitch Keegan wanted.

I hurry back to the woods, tears shifting in my eyes. I wish I didn't care. I wish I wasn't so close to Aaron. I don't want him to see me lose my shit. We hurry through the woods together, Aaron huffing and puffing.

"That motherfucker," he whispers. "I could fucking kill him."

I feel abandoned. Alone. The one person who saw those dark parts of me betrayed me.

I hear a cry come from the shed.

I stop, and Aaron and I turn back.

"God, he must be loving it," Aaron mutters with spite.

Then I hear another scream. An audible, "Help!"

A million thoughts beg for my attention, but I don't have time to process them. All I know is that Ian is in trouble and Roger is a fucking dead man. I race back to the shed. Not thinking. Hardly breathing. In what feels like a moment, I grab the back of Roger's polo, yank him off Ian, and throw him onto the concrete floor. He glances around like he doesn't even know where the fuck he is. When he looks to me, he doesn't even seem to know who I am. Let alone know what he's been doing to Ian.

I keep my eyes on him as I untie Ian and remove the gag from his mouth. He coughs and spits vomit across the wall before him. Then he collapses against me.

"Ian?" I ask.

He appears nearly as disoriented as Roger. His eyes wander about like he's having a hard time figuring out where he is. His face is bright red. He trembles against me like he's about to have a seizure. He heaves, then vomits. The mess runs down my arm as I hold him close. I help him sit on the floor and turn to Roger, who's still looking around like he's trying to make sense of what's going on.

"You're Aaron's boy," he says as though he's just now realizing who Ian is. He starts to his feet, his shorts at his ankles. As he tries to take a step, he trips on them and falls back to the floor.

Aaron hurries into the shed. "Roger? You sick shit!"

Roger glances around as if he's surrounded by an army of invisible demons, and Aaron kicks him in the face so that he rolls against the wall.

AARON

These bitches really fucked everything up, so I have to revise my plan.

Brad's pissed and has enough rage in him to take things too far. Especially on the guy who he believes took things too far with his pet boy. If I can encourage him to unleash that rage on Roger while I pump Ian full of this suxamethonium chloride, then I can convince him that whatever Roger slipped him before dragging him out here must've killed him. Same ending. Just a little more inconvenient than I anticipated. I can fix this. I just need to make sure Roger doesn't say a damn thing.

I drop onto my knees and punch him in his face repeatedly. A few hits in, and it's clear that my efforts combined with how fucking baked he is will do the trick.

Brad hurries over, squats down, and grabs Roger by his shirt collar. He pulls him to his feet and forces him against the opposite wall, knocking a rake and shovel to the floor. He curses Roger has he lays into him.

I hurry to Ian, retrieving the syringe from my pocket. He trembles as he presses his palm against the wall. He's definitely out of it enough that I can get away with this without Brad noticing. But as he turns to me, his disoriented expression sharpens.

"Everything's going to be okay," I say, lowering my voice to keep him from feeling alarmed. I kneel beside him.

He stirs and jumps to his feet, moving around me cautiously, though unsteadily. Like he's about to trip.

"Brad!" he calls. The sound of Brad pelting Roger fills the shed.

"Brad, help!"

"What are you talking about?" I ask.

"What's wrong?" Brad asks, dropping Roger so that he falls limp onto the floor.

"He brought me out here," Ian says. "Aaron did."

"He's out of it," I say to Brad. "Roger obviously doped him up with something. Look at how he's moving."

Ian holds his hands out before him. Like he's trying to balance just to stay on his feet.

Brad looks to Roger, who rolls around on the floor, moaning in pain.

"He did all this!" Ian exclaims as he tries to point to me, but ends up pointing at the door.

I approach him quickly and snatch his arm. "I'll get him back to the house."

He struggles against me, but he's weak from the roofie Jesse slipped him. I maintain my grip and force him with me toward the door.

"Brad, please!"

Brad steps in my path.

If he tries to stop me, he'll end up pumped full of this shit because right now, he's the strongest. The one I'll have the hardest time taking out. I can handle the defeated Roger and drugged Ian on my own. And if I have to kill them all, I will.

It looks like I won't have my sweet revenge on Brad after all.

IAN

I pry Aaron's hand off my arm. "It's him," I say. "He brought me here."

Brad eyes me suspiciously. I'm sure it's because of how out of it I still am, which is fair because I'm liable to fall over any second now.

Roger shuffles about on the floor.

Aaron looks like he's about to jump at me. He turns to Brad. "You saw what Roger did to him. He's fucking confused."

"Ian, Aaron didn't do anything to you," Brad says.

"He roofied me. I passed out, but I woke up for a moment, and he was carrying me out here. Roger may have done it, but Aaron's the one who brought me here. They're at least working together."

"He's lost it," Aaron says. "Look at him. He's still hopped up on whatever Roger drugged him with. Ian, you must have dreamt that."

Brad eyes Aaron uncertainly.

"Are you fucking kidding me?" Aaron asks. "After everything I've done for you, you're going to stand there and think that I had something to do with this? I'm not the sicko. I'm not the one who fucking...you know what you did. And I had your fucking back, so have mine for once in your fucking life."

"He didn't have your back," I say. "Aaron, tell him about Keegan's letter."

I turn to where I was tied up. My pants are on the floor, tucked in the corner. If I can show Brad that letter, he'll have to believe there's more to all this than me being hopped up on some drug. I head for my pants, working hard to navigate as the world seems to keep moving around me.

"Brad, what the fuck?" Aaron asks. "I don't know what that kid's talking about. Do you really think I would do this to you?"

I fetch the letter and take it to Brad, stumbling and struggling through a haze. As Brad reviews it, Aaron approaches him. "Brad, don't believe this kid."

Aaron pulls something out of his pocket. A syringe. I call to Brad, but not before Aaron's sticks him with whatever that shit is.

"No!" I shout. I don't have time to think, so I just leap forward, tackling Aaron to the floor so that I fall on top of him, beside Roger, who's still recovering from his injuries. I thrash about wildly. As much as I had the upper hand in my initial attack, one blow from Aaron knocks me to his side. He rolls on top of me and throws another punch that makes the shed spin around even more than it already is. As he's about to hit me with another, Brad grabs him and pulls him off me. They wrestle as I struggle to get to my feet. I have to help Brad, but considering the state I'm in, I'm not of much use to anyone right now.

Brad throws a punch that knocks Aaron against the wall. Aaron falls to the floor.

"What is fucking wrong with you?" Brad shouts. He starts toward him, but stumbles and collapses. "What the fuck did you stick me with?"

Aaron stands and heads for Brad.

I search around for the syringe. It's a few feet away from me. Mostly full. If the little bit that Aaron got into Brad was enough to do this to him, what's left has got to be enough to stop Aaron too.

I pick it up as Aaron turns and grabs a shovel from the corner of the shed. He starts for Brad.

"You fucking asshole," he says. "Did you think you could run around behind my back over and over again and get away with it? I'm not an idiot! But you are. You're so fucking easy to play, it's ridiculous."

I run at him, but as he notices me, he redirects the shovel's path and strikes me in the arm. The power of the blow knocks me to the floor. I check my hand for the syringe, but it isn't there. Must've dropped it when he hit me, which doesn't surprise me considering what little control I have over my body right now.

Aaron stoops down before me and picks the syringe up off the floor.

"Did you really think you could take me on, you piece of shit pledge? Who the fuck did you think you were?"

I'm in too much pain to have to deal with this on my own. But it's clear that Roger and Brad can't help.

"You ruined all this. You're the reason it all went to shit."

He kneels beside me and sticks the needle in my neck.

"Fuck!"

I imagine him fucking me and how much I never even wanted it. How he filled me again and again when all I wanted was Brad.

My thoughts drift back to my brother Jacob. Me standing over him, looking into his eyes as he stared off. The eerie part of it all was that, even though I understood what happened, a part of me felt like he would shake back to life at any moment.

That's what I was going to look like soon.

My dark desire—to end all the pain and suffering—resurfaces. Maybe Aaron could be my savior. The one who frees me from the unbearable stings of existence.

But as I see Brad lying across the floor, motionless, I know I have to live. Not for me, but for him.

"We had some good times, at least," Aaron says, offering a kiss on my cheek, his hand tense against the syringe.

"Fuck you," I say as I kick him in the crotch so hard that his hands instinctively retreat to aid his balls.

I grab the syringe and yank it out of my neck.

This is my last chance. I lunge at Aaron. He gazes at me horror-struck as I drive it into his eye and squeeze. He grabs my forearm and struggles against me, screaming out as I pump him full of a few ounces of the shit. He slams a fist into my face and knocks me back.

I throw up across the floor again. Still screaming out, Aaron pulls the syringe from his eye and tosses it aside.

I look to Brad who trembles on the ground. He needs help.

Aaron starts for me again when he stumbles—just the way Brad did—and collapses onto the floor.

I shiver. Adrenaline rushes through me, my body warring with whatever drug continues to disorient me.

Aaron lies still, his body shifting slightly until it finally stills. I look into his lifeless eye. It reminds me of Jacob. That look. That feeling that it isn't over. Even though I know it is.

Epilogue

Ian

As Brad grips onto my throat, the pressure in my head swells. My body demands air, but I resist its primal desires. All I need is to snap my fingers twice—our safety signal—and Brad will release me, but I don't want him to. He gazes down at me, his face locked in an angry glare. Like he's not fucking *me*, but an enemy.

I love it. Despite the new therapist I'm seeing, I've found I can't shake this dark desire that lingers within me.

My wrists bound to his headboard in Velcro cuffs, I shake on the bed as he fucks me like the god he is. A bead of sweat streams down his face and slides over the beauty mark on his cheek—the perfect complement to that magnificent face.

He releases my throat and grabs my nipples, squeezing tight. It hurts like fucking hell, but in just the right way.

He leans down and spits across my face, and I lick my lips to get what I can inside me. He spits again directly into my mouth. Then he releases one of my nipples and shoves his thumb in my mouth, grinding the saliva into my gums until I taste iron. I suck on his thumb the way I would suck on a cock.

It's been over a month since Aaron's attempted murder. Since I killed him when I pumped him full of that shit he stuck Brad with.

The police reopened the investigation into Keegan Rafferty's death. Roger's and Brad's statements; the letter that the police determined was a fake; and the bondage gear and drugs discovered in Aaron's dorm room, have convinced investigators that Aaron played a major role in Keegan's death. And even though Brad confessed his part in covering up the murder, after what Aaron did to me that night, the investigators suspect Brad was drugged and framed so that Aaron could manipulate him into helping cover up his crime. As for Roger, the DA isn't pressing charges against him for assaulting me, as we discovered through his and Jesse's statements that he was just as much a pawn in Aaron's sadistic games as Brad. Roger assured me it was too dark for him to recognize me from earlier that night, and while I believe him and agree it wasn't his fault, that knowledge can't take away how violated that experience has left me feeling. At least I won't have to face him again.

Since the incident, his family discovered his secret, and he's been withdrawn from Rayden. Rumor has it his parents sent him to an anti-gay camp. The media's passed around a lot of rumors since the discovery of the new evidence surrounding Keegan Rafferty's death, and it's been a PR nightmare for Alpha Theta Mu.

I tug at the cuffs as Brad grips tight onto my thighs and forces into me.

For the first few weeks after the assault, I had Brad inside me repeatedly. Taking me. Filling me with his fingers. I hoped if he could be rough enough, he could scrape off the flesh that Roger violated, but I can't be free of that experience. It haunts me just like my brother's face haunts me. And now Aaron's too.

I know Jesse still feels like crap about his part in it all, and although I told him it wasn't his fault—that he was manipulated by Aaron—our friendship is over. Not just because of what he did to me, but because of what I did to him.

Energy rushes through me in powerful waves as Brad slams into my prostate. He claws at my flesh, drawing pink marks where he scratches.

It feels so good. So right. He's everything I've ever needed in a man.

He grips my throat again and squeezes.

The hate in his expression is more severe tonight than usual. The horror of that night has only intensified how brutal he's been with me.

His grip tightens and my body wiggles in protest. The pressure that swells in my head feels as good as it always does. It makes me think of how nice it would be if he held on just a little too long.

A selfish, dark desire fills me as I feel a wave of energy rush into my cheeks.

I ball my hands into fists to fight myself from offering the signal. He'll be so mad if he catches on to what I'm up to, but this is what I've always wanted from him. He can free me. He can give me the ease I so desperately crave.

Blue and black spots dance before me.

They call to me.

Brad is just angry enough that I believe he doesn't realize how far he's going. I need to hold out a little longer. If this doesn't work, he'll be so mad, but this is the perfect opportunity. Through our other encounters, I've convinced him that I'll offer the signal before things go too far. I've led him to believe it's safe for him to unleash his darkness on me. And I've seen how much effort it requires for him to snap out of his state once I offer the signal.

This is my moment.

The spots before me, shifting through a range of colors, grow larger as I feel myself steadily losing consciousness. A rush of excitement fills me. Better than any high I've ever experienced. Better than even the most powerful climax with Brad.

It isn't the promise of relief for a moment, but forever.

Break me, Brad. Save me from all the pain. Save me from this nightmare.

THE END

About the Author

Devon McCormack

A good ole Southern boy, Devon McCormack grew up in the Georgia suburbs with his two younger brothers and an older sister. At a very young age, he spun tales the old fashioned way, lying to anyone and everyone he encountered. He claimed he was an orphan. He claimed to be a king from another planet. He claimed to have supernatural powers. He has since harnessed this penchant for tall tales by crafting worlds and characters that allow him to live out whatever fantasy he chooses. Devon is an out and proud gay man living with his partner in Atlanta, Georgia.